THE AUTHENTIC LEADER AS SERVANT (ALS)

ALS II COURSE 8
RESPONSIBILITY LEADERSHIP
Attributes, Principles, and Practices

SYLVANUS N. WOSU, Ph.D

THE AUTHENTIC LEADER AS SERVANT
ALS II COURSE 8
Developing Responsibility Leadership Attributes, Principles, and Practices

© Copyright 2024 by Sylvanus N. Wosu Ph.D.

Printed in the United States of America
ISBN: 978-1-960224-88-0

All rights reserved. No part of this book may be reproduced or transmitted in any form or by any means, electronic or mechanical, including photocopying, recording, or by any information storage and retrieval system, without permission in writing from the copyright owner.

Bible quotations are from the New King James (NKJV) version of the Bible unless otherwise indicated.

Other versions used in this book are the New International Version (NIV), New Living Translation (NLT), King James Version (KJV), English Standard Version (ESV), and Good News Translation (GNT). Unless otherwise specified, NKJV should be assumed.

The views expressed in this work are solely those of the author and do not necessarily reflect the views of the publisher, and the publisher disclaims any responsibility for them.

To order additional copies of this book, contact:
Proisle Publishing Services LLC
39-67 58th Street, 1st floor
Woodside, NY 11377, USA
Phone: (+1 646-480-0129)
info@proislepublishing.com

TABLE OF CONTENTS

FOREWORD — XI
ACKNOWLEDGMENTS — XV
DEDICATION — XVII
PREFACE — 19
    About Leader As Servant Leadership (LSL) Model — 22
    About the Authentic Leader as Servant (ALS) — 25
    About the ALS Courses — 26

CHAPTER 1
UNDERSTANDING LEADERSHIP ATTRIBUTES — 35
    Functional Definitions — 35
    Comparisons With Other Works — 40
    Principle of Leadership Attribute — 42
    Authentic Leadership Attributes — 43
    Summary 1 Understanding Leadership Process — 48

CHAPTER 2
RESPONSILITY LEADERSHIP ATTRIBUTE — 51
    Characteristics of Responsibility Attribute — 52
    Principle of Leadership Responsibility Attribute — 58
    Summary 2 Developing Responsibility Leadership Attribute — 60

CHAPTER 3
DEVELOPING RESPONSIBLITY-OBLIGATION — 61
    Summary 3 Developing Responsibility-Obligation — 69

CHAPTER 4
DEVELOPING RESPONSIBILITY- WILLINGNESS — 71
    How to Increase the Will to Act — 73
    Summary 4 Developing Responsibility-Willingness — 74

CHAPTER 5
DEVELOPING RESPONSIBILITY-ACCOUNTABILITY — 77
    Summary 5 Developing Responsibility-Accountability — 80

CHAPTER 6
 DEVELOPING ACCOUNTABILITY-QUALITY 81
   Reasons for Establishing Accountability --------------------------------------- 84
   Summary 6 Developing Accountability-Quality --------------------------------- 85

TOPIC INDEX 87
REFERENCES 89

Foreword

The modern world today is obsessed with standardization and modalities. As a result, in the realm of leadership, many books have spout associated leadership theories and models and explain them as the path to follow. However, the critical dimensions that distinguish the effectiveness of any leadership process are the values and attribute the leader brings to the table; desired change is influenced by leadership styles or standards. These many standards and theories of leadership often are not in step with the changing times or the followers' needs. The trend is a bit like stocking different kinds of foods in a grocery store and expecting that they will meet everybody's needs the same way and at all times. Aisles are packed with varieties of food with expiration dates in the future, but getting the best deal on the products is what really matters to those who buy and use the products

In many ways, this is the state of leadership in the modern world. Increasingly, even leaders of public institutions are tasked with turning a profit for themselves or the organization they serve. The idea of a "leader" seems to float uneasily alongside the ranks of fundraisers or profit raisers in contrast to any kind of role model for followers or employees. That which is knowable, measurable, and marketable has surpassed the difficult intangibility of strong moral leadership attributes as the central guideline for achievement and success.

In this complicated space, Dr. Sylvanus Wosu introduces his complex idea of the Leader as a Servant Leadership, which is in this book, modeled on Christian tradition. Like all intricate ideas, Dr. Wosu's central point depends on a paradox: a person is best qualified to lead when he or she is most ready to serve. This paradox has been monopolized rhetorically by "public servants" who often serve either self-interest or the interests of specific lobbies. The Authentic Leader as Servant penetrates past the superficial concept of "serving" and details the internal state of true servitude or Servanthood.

While the book is primarily focused on the Christian model of leadership attributes such as discipleship, empathy, affection, and Servanthood, it does so not merely on the grounds of blind faith, but rather via numerous contemporary sociological and business-driven studies on how leaders should seek a leader-follower relationship that is simultaneously productive and nurturing. Dr. Wosu's most piercing insights always involve this secular–Christian dialogue. This book demonstrates that Christ's model for leadership is one that may exist successfully outside the confines of a faith relationship; it places the values of Christ's religious significance in leadership at the center of the framework. It is clear from Dr. Wosu's generous own life story of faith—a faith tested by humbling difficulties—is at the center of both his orientation and motivation for writing.

In language that is so concise, it is often illustrated in mathematical formulas; Dr. Wosu explains the deep structural integrity of Christ's Leader as the Servant Leadership model. One could imagine leaders of any doctrine benefiting from the analyses contained in these pages. The book's message repeatedly encourages the reader to imagine a scenario or reflect on memories and personal experiences to prove or test its many points. Thus, the book depends on a form of praxis, a lesson that could be or has been enacted, by the participating reader. I am very impressed at the volume and level of thinking of the author. Parts of the book involve his personal story, which is especially riveting. I cannot imagine what he had to endure, which he referred to as a" wilderness walk," to accomplish the goal he set for himself. His life stories on these pages are inspiring and stimulating.

In this way, the text eschews dogmatism in favor of the self-discovery Socratic Method of teaching and learning. The reader is not badgered into complying with a religious objective but is rather asked to consider the applicability of difficult biblical concepts in relation to modern life. It is a fascinating and very thought-provoking read.

Hence, the book does not seek to make the leader a servant, a cookie-cutter corporate buzzword, but rather asks the reader to imagine him or herself interacting with a range of concepts. One of Dr. Wosu's great strengths is his reservation when it comes to forcing his reading's interpretation on the material he presents.

The book parallels Biblical and modern leadership scenarios in ways that consistently provoke thought, and while it is clear Dr. Wosu has his particular leadership style; the space for the reader's own thoughts is always left open.

The book could not have been written in any other way with integrity. Its format and formulas are offered to the reader of the leader as a servant role that it analyzes in its pages. To find a text that instructs from this humble position is profoundly refreshing in a genre that is often packaged inside a cover with a sizeable picture of the "modest" author, smiling egotistically beneath a name spelled out in large, gold lettering. Throughout its pages, this text feels as if it serves the reader.

In the end, this is the most satisfying aspect of the book. There is no standardized approach to achieving successful leadership. There is no promise of power and a bigger payday; in fact, the book often proffers just the opposite. The reader is not encouraged to devalue the experience of leadership by finding some economic metric for marking success but is rather asked to think deeply about the most basic elements of internal and social interaction within the framework of a Christian tradition. What this means will be different for every reader. Indeed, even in the context of single chapters, I found myself questioning or re-evaluating moments of my own life. This book serves; it doesn't feel like filling in multiple-choice questions, staring at a wall of flavorless grocery products, or hearing the endless servant promises of today's political scene. It feels like a humble invitation to consider a single paradoxical element of a profoundly productive tradition.

-Tobias Bates

Acknowledgments

A book on leadership attributes as aspects of Servant Leadership sprouted from the wealth of knowledge and the inspirations of many other leaders. Their writings were sources of inspiration, challenges, and examples of excellence to emulate. I acknowledge the leaders listed below for their help in one way or the other. I am very grateful and I hereby express my appreciation and thanks:

Mr. Wayne Holt, introduced me first to the subject of Servanthood in one of our Stephen Ministerial Training classes, and he is the one who has conducted his life as a leader–servant; he encouraged me throughout my writing;

Dr. Harvey Borovetz, Distinguished Professor and Chair of the Bioengineering Department, is a leader-servant in many ways, he modeled Servanthood and encouragement attributes throughout his leadership in an academic setting.

Dr. Clifford and Dr. Patience Obih, in so many measures exemplified the practical leadership attributes discussed in this book.

Pastor Lance Lecocq, Lead Pastor of Monroeville Assembly of God, for his excellent model of servanthood, empowerment, and emulation attributes to the ministerial team, I am thankful for his motivation and encouragement throughout the several hours on this project;

To my administrative assistant, Ms. Terri Cook, who was always the first to review the manuscript; I am very grateful for her dedication.

To the African Christian Fellowship USA, institutions, and all other organizations where I have served in one leadership capacity or the other, thank you for affording me senior leadership positions that provided the leadership platform and opportunities to grow as a leader.

Dr. Lawrence Owoputi, a brother I am proud to call my friend; for his dedication to serving others, his generosity, healing care, and responsibility attributes during our term in office and in chapter leadership positions; he taught me that excellent following is also part of good leadership;

To Tobias Bates, for his editorial work on the original draft of the book, and his dedication to completing the work.

Mr. Edward F. Kondis, a member of our Engineering Board of Visitors, for his always encouraging and moral support;

Dr. Enefaa N. Wosu, my wife and life partner, for her love, commitment, and prayer support, especially during those long night hours I was not there for her and her constant reminder of who I must be as a leader-servant. Without her support, forbearance, wisdom, and encouragement, this project would not have been completed; I say, thank you very much.

And to God alone be all the glory and honor for the divine inspiration and guidance in initiating and completing this life-transforming book project.

DEDICATION

I humbly submit this book back unto the gracious hands of God who inspired the writings through His Holy Spirit!

I dedicate this book to my virtuous wife of 45 years, Rev. (Dr.) Enefaa Wosu whose spiritual leadership is an important gateway to our home, and to our four wonderful children—Prof. Eliada Wosu-Griffin EL, HeCareth, Tamuno-Emi, and Chidinma. From them all, I learnt what it meant to be a leader-servant. I could not be blessed with better teachers.

PREFACE

What characteristics did Biblical leaders like the Apostle Paul, Moses, Joshua, and Nehemiah as servants of their people display outwardly that distinguished them from other leaders, both then and now? The Apostle Paul kept his focus to *emulate* Christ and endured all the infirmities and persecutions he suffered to complete his goal to preach the gospel of Jesus Christ. He inspired Timothy and others through his effective *discipleship* leadership to imitate him as he emulated Christ. Moses' outward display of his *trust* in God's power earned him a good level of trust from the people and empowered him for the mission of delivery of God's children from bondage in Egypt; he had to *reproduce* himself in Joshua to complete the mission. But the greatest of them was Jesus Christ, who humbly sacrificed His life to finish the work of redemption. In His *Servanthood*, commitment, and love for the people, He became the ultimate *model* of a leader as a servant to *emulate*.

Let's consider for a moment secular leaders in these current times! For example, think of Henry Ford, who founded the successful Ford Motor Company; Bill Gates who created the global empire that is Microsoft; Albert Einstein, who in many ways is synonymous with a genius for his contributions to modern physics; Abraham Lincoln, remembered as one of the greatest presidents and leaders of United States; and many others like these we cannot mention. What did all these leaders have in common? What propelled them to turn their initial failures or challenges into eventual successes? None had a direct mentor or inherited any fortune from their parents. Nevertheless, they all eventually succeeded. These people can be distinguished from others based on their self-will to succeed, their self-confidence and belief in themselves, their self-determination, and their perseverance, among other characteristics. The distinguishing characteristics displayed externally in service or relationships toward others are the outward functional attributes that define that leader.

Think about yourself as a student, faculty member, or that new executive. What was it that made your journey to success different and even great? Students and colleagues, when they see or hear about my display of what I have referred to as the 'wilderness walk of faith', have asked me to share the critical attitudinal elements that made me remain inwardly resilient and undaunted and yet outwardly joyful in the difficulties I had faced. This book is the result of those reflections. Let me explain one such teaching moment.

Many years ago, sitting in my research lab on a Saturday morning trying to finish writing my dissertation, a fellow graduate student walked into the room to talk with me. He was contemplating terminating his graduate studies. He was a privileged single male student but felt the load was just too much.

"Sylvanus," he asked, with seriousness in his eyes, "your research advisor suggested that I should ask you, 'what is it that makes you tick?'.'What is it about you that makes you joyful and at peace with yourself and determined to finish, no matter the situations and high expectations we face in this department?"

What he asked me were deeply reflective questions, but I was willing and excited to answer them. Even so, before I do, let's look at the context. At that period in my life, I had four little children as a graduate student; in fact, more children than any of the faculties at that time, except for one faculty member who had eight children. I received little or no support from the department. I was then an international alien, did not qualify for financial aid, and was not given any research assistant position. I was, therefore, self-supported with two off-campus part-time jobs. I joked at being a minority of minorities, the only student in the department with such a label,—but I was self-willed to succeed. My adaptability attribute, coupled with perseverance and resilience, was all that I needed to succeed despite the odds against me. In every exam, homework assignment, or project I had to compete with students with full financial aid, plus they had nothing to distract their attention from their studies. I lived with the attitude that using disadvantages as an excuse was not an option. Aspiring to earn my Ph.D. was a life dream, and I was willing to give my ultimate best to actualize that dream even in the face of challenges. The choice was mine!

So I looked at my classmate and all I could see was a student striding through a valley through which I also walked. He needed me to show him how to walk the walk, to empathize with him. To answer his question, I smiled, not that I wanted to, but because it was just who I was. The joy he attributed to me was an overflow of my appreciation of God's grace that His life in me was externally manifesting His light to bless someone else. It was a great teaching moment; I capitalized on it to tell my classmate that my joy was not about me. He could see physically but about He who was in me, he could not see in the flesh; I needed him to know that I was just showing forth His life in me. At first, my classmate did not understand the spiritual prose or metaphor I was using. He looked surprised but open to hearing more.

I did not ask if he was a Christian. However, right on my desk was my small green pocket Bible. I opened to 2 Corinthians 12:9 (NIV) and handed it to him to read. As he read the passage: "But he said to me, 'My grace is sufficient for you, for my power is made perfect in weakness.' Therefore, I will boast all the more gladly about my weaknesses, so that Christ's power may rest on me," I noticed how absorbed he was in the words

He looked astonished and read it again, this time silently. "This is interesting, but what does this mean?" He asked. I took his question to mean, "How does this relate to my question?

I explained to my friend that the external attitudes he or my advisors saw in me that warranted the question, "What makes you tick" were inspired by my inner value system based on my faith in this same Christ and His teachings. My desire to manifest His life and self-confidence is all because of what He has promised in His word if I believed. I have believed His words and have gained self-determination and faith to make the right choices through Him for my life, and his spirit has given me perseverance and resilience to focus on finishing strong in pursuit of any goal. "With that faith, I have continued, more passionately and excitedly; I can look at my challenges and vulnerabilities and delight joyfully in them, even as an alien minority of minorities! His grace and power have empowered me to do all things I want to do. That is what makes me tick," I explained.

He looked at me as if he got his answer. "Wow, thanks!" he said, looking inspired and ready to face his challenges. As we concluded with a prayer, and he stood up to leave, I pointed empathetically to his face and said, "If I made it despite my challenges, you have absolutely no excuse but to persevere to complete your studies; you can make it too!"

It is fitting to report that this encounter with my classmate transformed his will and determination to continue. Yes, he was encouraged and went on to complete his graduate studies. He emulated self-will and perseverance from the example of the most vulnerable of all students in the department.

The inner value system of a Leader-Servant is founded not only on his faith but his self-will, coupled with self-leadership; it is the greatest mentor who can turn any situation into an inconceivable success. Self-will is the primary driver for determination, resilience, and perseverance. It is what wakes you up in the morning to ask for strength to do whatever it is you are setting out to do. Based on my life walk of faith, I can state with absolute certainty that faith is the unseen assuredness that can empower you to turn your life's probable impossibilities into great and improbable possibilities.

ABOUT LEADER AS SERVANT LEADERSHIP (LSL) MODEL

Looking at the testimony above, do you know the source that energizes the characteristics you display outside and how your inner self is related to what others see outside? What distinguishes you from others is what combines to define your attributes! As a follower, can you identify the characteristics that distinguish your leaders? As an executive, how do you base your evaluation of yourself? Or how do you evaluate that brand-new manager or new youth director you want to hire? To what do you compare the individual's qualities when you look at his CV? What is the basis of your measure? Do you know if you are a substantial leader? These personal questions and much more are the subjects of this two-volume book, 'The Authentic Leader as Servant Part I: The Outward Leadership Attributes, Principles, and Practices', is written in two parts; the second part 'The Leader as Servant Leadership Model. Part II'; deals with the Inner Strength Leadership Attributes, Principles, and Practices.

When we think about today's corporate greed, deepening divide between the haves and have-not, gridlock in political systems, conflicts and wars, high divorce rates, and the rich young ruler in the Bible, it is easy to agree that all these people share a few things in common: self-centeredness, pride, lack of compassion, and greed. There is a great need in today's suffering world for leader-servants who display leadership attributes. These attributes should be oriented toward selfless service to others. Indeed, our world is increasingly drifting away from global serving reality toward the self and apathy. The most credible message or model for a possible solution to this dilemma and the answer to several complex leadership questions can be found in the foundation of the ultimate leader-servant, Jesus Christ. This book defines the Leader as Servant Leadership attribute as the combined acts of two or more distinctive functional leadership characteristics exhibited in service and relationship toward others. There is no better time than now for a book that presents comprehensive and irrevocable facts and principles regarding how to develop effective attributes of the leader-servant.

The Leader as Servant Leadership Model

My first book on this subject, The Leader as Servant Leadership Model, explains that Jesus' servant leadership model is based on the notion of a Leader as a Servant and not on a Servant as Leader. There are four distinct differences between a Servant as Leader (Servant-leader) and the Leader as Servant (leader--servant) models. It is pertinent to highlight them here to connect to this book, Authentic Leader as Servant.

A Leader as Servant is a leader first. The leader–servant as a leader does not in the line of duty go projecting or lording his or her power and authority over others but is the person to lead the process of influencing desired changes in others through his humble example of being a servant or having a serviceable attitude toward others. He or she is a serving leader, not a lording leader. He leads as a servant by putting others' needs above his own needs and rights. Jesus emphasized the word "as" meaning that the leader (the Master) chooses to serve as a servant even though he is the leader. A leader–servant emulates Jesus, who gave up all rights, and emptied and expended Himself on His followers. He empowered them to become more like Him. A leader-servant is known as a leader first but is seen as a great leader by his humble attendant heart and acts of service to others. His greatness comes from his ability to put others above himself.

Leader as Servant is a Biblical Concept. The model or image of a humble serving leader motivated Jesus' disciples to see that if their master could do this for them, they must also be able to do it for others. Jesus clearly demonstrated the process of leader-as-servant leadership. In some cases, He chose to serve by leading when He wanted to create the image or model of the leader-servant in certain acts. In other cases, He chose to lead by serving, when he showed care and empathy toward the people and led the disciples to see empathy as a leadership attribute.

Leader as Servant is an Authentic Leadership Model to follow. The Leader as the Servant leadership model intentionally positions Jesus as an original model of a leader to follow.

He was serving His disciples to demonstrate that the process of becoming a great leader was earned through humble acts of service to others; He made them understand that He was empowering them to succeed Him as leader-servants through service to others. The result was an incomparable legacy of leadership that changed their communities. The fact that Jesus relinquished his rights or shared His power did not diminish His power and influence. In fact, his influence increased at least 11 X 100%, if we ignore the one case of Judas.

The Leader as Servant Transforms Organizational Culture. The proposed LSL model seeks to transform and sustain the community or organization by instilling key leadership values or "leadership presence" among followers or an organization's members. Change is sustained when everyone in the organization takes ownership of the change. Rather than focusing on leading more followers to be great followers who conform to the organizational culture, LSL seeks to lead and empower better leaders to be distinguished leaders and community builders.

There are four distinctions, which clearly differentiate many of the existing servants as Leader-based philosophies in relation to servant leadership from my LSL model. Even in the corporate or institutional worlds, there is nothing better than Jesus on which to base Servant Leadership. There is nothing more authentic and impacting than the servant leadership modeled by the life and teachings of Jesus Christ.

The LSL model uses exploratory questions, scenarios, and graphic visualizations to excite critical thinking in ways no other book on this subject has yet attempted. Several personal testimonies of my wilderness walk of faith with God are used to connect the reader to real-life experiences of the concepts discussed. The riveting effect is that the text engages and encourages the reader to walk through the experiences presented. The aim is to inspire the reader spiritually, mentally, and professionally with this far-reaching exposition on the subject of servant leadership.

ABOUT THE AUTHENTIC LEADER AS SERVANT (ALS)

The *Authentic Leader as Servant* argues that no leadership model is as authentic, other-centered, able to build communities, and productive and service-oriented as the model of our ultimate leader-servant, Jesus Christ. No source can provide a better point of reference than that provided in the Bible. Hence, this book aims to be more than just a text on leadership; it hopes to be a personal discovery for those who aspire to develop effective leadership attributes that grow leaders as servants who ultimately develop thriving other-centered communities. This book presents a comprehensive, biblically-based study regarding how to develop these attributes and how they are applied in a servant leadership process. In this biblical context and for clarity, Servant Leadership means *Leader-as-Servant Leadership*. A *leader-servant* refers to a *leader as a servant*, which is distinct from a servant-leader or servant as leader.

Leader as Servant Leadership attributes are shaped by the Leadership's Inner Value system, which consists of character, motivation, and commitment. The *Authentic Leader as Servant* is presented as a necessary resource to complement my *The Leader as Servant Leadership (LSL) Model*. The LSL model integrates a transformative leadership framework and interactive dimensions of Servant Leadership. Leader as Servant Leadership is a process in which a leader, in his leadership position, purposefully chooses to put others' rights and needs above his positional rights and personal needs. He then serves, enables, and empowers followers for growth that builds a thriving organization. The LSL model looks at the predominant Servant Leadership concepts and shares how they compare with biblical principles on how we should lead and be led.

ABOUT THE ALS COURSES

The three books, *LSL Model* and *The Authentic Leader as Servant* (Parts I and II), together demonstrate that with today's global visions to reach people of all races and cultures, now is the time for an authentic servant's heart of service. Those visions and the leadership processes are most effective with the appropriate leadership attributes centered more on people than on the organization, principles regarding how to develop effective attributes of leader-servant.

The ALS I and II combined presented twenty leaders as servant leadership attributes. The series of ALS courses supply training guide to understand, develop, and practice the attributes in a leadership process. Each course is independent and self-contained and does not depend on completing any other course in the series of 20 courses. It is, however strongly recommended, in fact a must read, that chapters 1 and 2 in each series be covered as they lay the foundation of LSL model on which ALS is based.

ALS (Parts I & II) Course Layout

The *Authentic Leader as Servant (ALS)* leadership (parts I and II) book has been broken down into 20 courses in workbook format to achieve three goals 1) Self-discovery of the acts of developing the attribute under review in the course, 2) deeper understanding of the principles, research and biblical teaching behind the attributes, and 3) Learning the strategies for practicing the attributes.

Instruction

The set of questions following each chapter are designed to serve as a guide to discover, explore, and practice the essential ALS leadership attributes, principles, and practices in leadership process. The questions are comprehensive review based on the content of this specific chapter only.

To maximize the learning outcomes, the learner must read through this chapter and sections. Some referenced scriptures in the book are repeated in the summaries for added review if needed, even though they were discussed in the section in which they apply.

PREFACE

> The exercises that follow each chapter will help you in not only understanding your own strength and weaknesses in your acts of the attribute but will guide you in developing practical strategies you can apply in self-leadership process or helping others grow in leadership
>
> All answers to the questions are contained in the associated chapter or sections; consultation of new sources, except for the reference scriptures, is not needed. Thus, it is expected that you answer the questions after you have read the associated section or chapter of the workbook. The scripture or other references cited are only for references as they already discussed in the book

ALS II Course 1: Adaptability Leadership Attribute—*Flexibility overcomes rigidity in new and changing situations.*

Adaptability is framed as an inner strength quality of a leader in responding to changing needs or situations in a service mission. According to the Army training Handbook, adaptability is "an individual's ability to recognize changes in the environment, identify the critical elements of the new situation, and trigger changes accordingly to meet new requirements." God showed Moses adaptability when he empowered him to use the rod in his hand as an instrument for the mission ahead of him. This course will attempt to give meanings to personal reflective questions to discover the distinguishing characteristics of Leadership Adaptability. Numerous techniques, personal examples, empirical case studies, and applications of the adaptability developing strategies are discussed concepts. Practice questions at the end of each chapter are used to guide your development and to frame meanings out of the content to improve your acts of adaptability in a leadership process.

ALS II Course 2: Courage Leadership Attribute—*Courage is the inner strength of the mind to triumph over paralyzing fears of purposeful action that yields good success*

Courage Leadership Attribute is the lynchpin of effective Servant Leadership that supports the display of all the other attributes? Having the inner strength of character and convictions to persevere and hold on to new and often misunderstood ideas in the face of opposition takes courage—inner strength to triumph over the fear of failure or danger. It is even greater courage to venture into positions or overcome situations that nobody like you, has gone to before or where many better qualified than you had gone and failed. In all cases, they all display courage in the face of obstacles and uncertainties. The success is more about courage than the experience. Can such courage be learned or inspired? How do leaders or successful people in their callings get to their heights of achievements? How can courage be an inner strength within or beyond leadership? How does courage attribute triumph over paralyzing fear? This course explores answers to these questions and more by searching for the distinguishing characteristics of courage. Numerous techniques, personal examples, empirical case studies, including practice questions at the end of each chapter are used to guide your development and to frame meanings out of the content to improve your acts of courage leadership process.

ALS II Course 3: Empathy Leadership Attribute—*A measure of a leader's compassion is the empathic engagement in a follower's experience and state of well-being beyond just expressions of feelings and concerns.*

Empathy attribute is the ability to project one's personality and experiences into another person's thoughts, emotions, direct experience, position, and act toward the wellness of that person. How can a leader walk along with someone in that individual's "wilderness" state of suffering or danger? What motivates a leader to *empathize* with a follower? How is empathy an inner strength leadership attribute? Whether it's in your church, your business, your institution, or in your community, this course provides a comprehensive biblical-based discussion on the role of a leader as a servant in empathizing with those he leads. The aim is to inspire the reader spiritually, mentally, and professionally with this far-reaching exposition on empathy in servant leadership. How can a leader make a lasting positive impact in the lives of those he or she leads? Answers to these and other personal reflective questions are explored in this course on Leadership Empathy Attributes. Numerous techniques, personal examples, empirical case studies, including practice questions at the end of each chapter are used to guide your development and to frame meanings out of the content to improve your acts of empathy leadership process.

ALS II Course 4: Encouragement Leadership Attribute—*The direct measures of encouragement are the inspired strength and quality of uplifted spirit to persevere toward a desired outcome.*

There are times when people want to grow in their potential, want to change their present situation, feel emotionally low in lived experiences, or feel as if they should be appreciated for a job well done. In any of these cases, some encouragement goes a long way to lift up the spirit of someone low. A case study is of the leadership qualities of Barnabas, named the "Son of Encouragement" by the disciples (Acts 4:36), because they saw him as an *encourager*. You can only be an encourager from the strength of your inner personality. The act of encouragement is mostly expressed or *given* to inspire growth or apply a spiritual gift to serve others. What did the disciples see in Barnabas? Obviously, he must have affected them with his acts of encouragement. They saw him as an encourager by his *courage* to *inspire* them at a time they desperately needed to move the ministry forward. This course explores the distinguishing characteristics of encouragement attributes in servant leadership. Each characteristic of encouragement attribute will be discussed in detail with emphasis on strategies of how they can be further developed or practiced by a leader-servant in a leadership process. Practice questions at the end of each chapter are used to guide your development and to frame meanings out of the content to improve your acts of encouragement leadership process.

ALS II Course 5: Initiation Leadership Attribute—*Initiation creates the catalyst for a vision, and the vision when acted upon, produces a desired change.*

The initiation of a process for a desired change is the core of the inner strength of a decisive leader in any leadership process. Initiation leadership is the act of taking step to originate or get something started. In general, initiative is an "individual's action that begins a process, often done without direct managerial influence." The primary outcome of the initiation attribute is that it leads to desired change; something new in the lives of the followers or organization, such as a new growth in followers, a new product or policy in an organization, or a new mission or mission agenda. How do leaders take action to begin a process of change? What are the distinguishing initiation characteristics of leaders such as Moses and Nehemiah in working according to God's agenda? How does a leader conceive a strategic vision for initiation action?. or negotiate his way to influence possible actions toward that vision. This course explores answers to these, and other questions based on examples from Nehemiah (Nehemiah 1:4 through 2:6-8) and Moses and God (Exodus 3 and 4:1-14).

ALS II Course 6: Listening Communication   Leadership Attribute
—*Effective communication occurs at the convergence of listening attention, hearing, and understanding of the information transmitted.*

A leader-servant face three important types of communication at one point or the other. At the core is listening ability as the inner strength and ability to receive and understand the meanings of words and messages internally and accurately in a two-way communication process. How does a leader-servant communication with God, the Holy Spirit, and followers (individually or collectively) to be most effective. The course explores how the three elements—words spoken, unspoken, and in the spirit—offer unique reflections of the communication process and what they share in common. How does listening serve as a critical element of effective communication between people forms the bridge by which a leader can be effective?. A leader's capacity to listen to communicate effectively depends on the leader's inner strength to perceive, hear, and understand the information from written, verbal, and non-verbal exchanges. Each characteristic of listening communications attribute will be discussed in detail with emphasis on strategies of how they can be further developed or practiced by a leader-servant. Practice questions at the end of each chapter are used to guide your development and to frame meanings out of the content to improve your acts of listening leadership process.

ALS II Course 7: Navigation Leadership Attribute—*Leaders who prepare for and chart through a purposeful course of action arrive with their followers at the desired destination.*

The navigation attribute is having a *vision* for the intended destination plus the direction to get there. Having a vision is a quality of the inner strength of a leader and the path that the leader follows in the life journey is often influenced by internal and external factors. The organizational culture and climate collectively combine to make an organization unique through the diversity of employees' characteristics, values, needs, attitudes, and expectations. How does a leader-servant *navigate* and *negotiate* his actions through the organization and people he serves, individually or collectively, to *finish* or *arrive* at his purpose? How do you prepare your followers to *finish* strong or *arrive* at their destinations? This course explores answers to these and other questions and how a leader's inner strength capacity can empower him to navigate the cultural bridges to influence the desired change in others in their personal and professional needs and attitudes.

ALS II Course 8: Responsibility Leadership Attribute—L*eadership responsibility is the measure of the quality of a Leader's accountability for the growth of followers and the organization*

Responsibility leadership refers to possessing the capability and accountability needed in the act of being responsible (trustworthy, dependable, honest, etc.) in a leadership process. At a personal level, it defines the level of your position (pastor, deacon, department head, janitor, etc.) in your church, family, or employment. Responsible leaders in their positions *choose* to emphasize the positive, uplifting, and flourishing side of organizational life. Are there qualities in your position that need to be trained or developed to influence positive outcomes in people and organizations? Organizationally, what are the attributes of the leadership structure, process, and culture that are most conducive for maximizing the growth of followers and organizations in service toward others? How can responsibility qualities be developed to enhance high-quality relationships, emotional competencies, positive communication, beneficial energy development, and positive climates for the effective leader as a servant leadership process? The course explores answers to these and other questions. Distinguishing leadership characteristics of responsibility attributes are identified and discussed in detail. Practice questions at the end of each chapter are used to guide your development and to frame meanings out of the content to improve your acts of responsibility leadership process.

ALS II Course 9: Stewardship Leadership Attribute—*A measure of good stewardship is the entrustments' better and richer growth change at the end than at the beginning*

ALS RESPONSIBILITY LEADERSHIP
ATTRIBUTES, PRINCIPLES, & PRACTICES

Stewardship leadership is the process of u*tilizing* and managing the resources entrusted to you by someone. We recognize that God has ownership of everything above, and below the earth. In that context, we are all stewards of what God owns, including our lives but entrusted to us to be managed and maintained in a purposeful manner that will honor God. What are the distinctive servant leadership characteristics of stewardship and how can they be developed? This course explores answers to these questions with reference to servant leadership. Practice questions at the end of each chapter are used to guide your development and to frame meanings out of the content to improve your acts of steward leadership process

ALS II Course 10: Vision Leadership Attribute—*You have a vision when you understand how you get to your mission-purpose and what the future outcome will be relative to your present.*

The vision leadership attribute gives the leader the ability to specify in the present *what* each follower's or group's growth should be in the future, *where* to focus these efforts to meet that growth; *how* he will accomplish all aspects of his mission, *which* future (destination) he aspires to lead the people, and *when* the purpose will be achieved. Leadership without direction leads followers to nowhere. Vision is the most common descriptor of effective leadership and must be clear and inspirational in order to achieve desired purpose. What are the qualities a visionary leader? When was the last time you added brand new challenges to your normal routine to achieve a new you? Answers to these and other questions are explored in this course. The primary characteristics of visionary leadership will be identified and used to frame a principle of leadership vision attribute. Practice questions at the end of each chapter are used to guide your development and to frame meanings out of the content to improve your acts of encouragement leadership process.

Referenced Scriptures

A variety of Bible translations from over 11,200 original Hebrew, Aramaic, and Greek words to about 6,000 English words do exist with variations in meanings and emphases. I am not a biblical scholar and do not pretend to be one; Hence, I have avoided researching the roots of these words and personally prefer New King James Version (NKJV). I have intentionally used other translations for three main reasons; first, to allow for increased impact and alignment of words to the most desired meaning and emphasis in the concepts being addressed. Second, I wanted new and personal discovery of meanings from translations with which I have not been familiar. And third, I wanted to allow readers who may desire translations other than the NKJV the benefit of their preferred translations. Hence, in addition to the NKJV, other translations used in the book include New International Version (NIV), New Living Translation (NLT), King James Version (KJV), English Standard Version (ESV), and Good News Translation (GNT). Unless otherwise specified, NKJV should be assumed.

Sylvanus Nwakanma Wosu

CHAPTER 1
UNDERSTANDING LEADERSHIP ATTRIBUTES

Leadership attribute is the combined acts of two or more distinctive functional leadership characteristics exhibited in service and relationship toward others.

The starting point of our discussion is the understanding of the key functional definitions and concepts that describe the theme of this book. In general, 1 will define leadership as an integrative process in which a person applies appropriate attributes to guide and influence the sought-after attitudinal changes in others toward accomplishing a particular goal. Specifically, the Leader as Servant Leadership is a process in which a leader intentionally chooses to put the follower's rights and needs above his positional rights and personal needs, and serves, enables, and empowers them for desired spiritual and professional growth that builds thriving communities.

FUNCTIONAL DEFINITIONS

In the context of these definitions, I will begin the descriptions of the leadership attributes of an authentic leader-servant by offering a functional definition of Leadership Attributes, and showing how that definition differs from those of Leadership Character, Characteristics, and Traits.

Leadership Character is the sum total of personal qualities in leadership, such as honesty, values, vision, trust, and so on that make up the moral capital of the leader; Leadership character should describe who the leader is inside or the leader's basic personality traits.

The Leadership Characteristics describe the distinctive characteristics or features of a leader, such as attitudes, competencies, skills, and specific experiences that go beyond his character (personality). Leadership characteristics determine how (through skills and competencies) the leader leads or take actions in the process of leadership in any particular situation;

The Leadership traits are the distinguishing leadership characteristics of a leader (these are things that define his leadership characteristics), which differentiate from personality traits... Leadership traits are the set of characteristics that define a particular leader's leadership. This means that a leadership characteristic is a trait when it is a unique characteristic of the leader.

Leadership Attributes, unlike leadership character, characteristics, and traits, is *a leadership attribute and the combined act of two or more distinctive functional leadership characteristics exhibited in service and relationship toward others* or traits externally displayed in action toward others. All leadership attributes grow out of the leadership inner value system but can be externally displayed predominantly as an outbound or outward attribute or both:

1. **Outbound Attributes:** These are distinctive outward-bound attributes emanating from the inner strength of the leader to support external conduct in service and relationships toward others. They form the internal core functional qualities that motivate or enhance the outward manifestation of the inside character toward others. The outbound attribute such as listening and vision, for example, are the direct results of the inner values of the leader such as patience, hearing, love, humility, or all the fruits of the spirit.

2. **Outward Attributes:** These are distinctive functional outward outer visible attributes emanating from the richness of the outbound and inner values of the leader. For example, external attributes such as Servanthood, emulation/modeling, empathy, etc. are outflows from the leader who will directly impact the follower. Outward attributes can be enriched by the outbound (inner) attributes. As shown in Figure 1, the outward attributes in general form the outer core of

CHAPTER 1
UNDERSTANDING LEADERSHIP ATTRIBUTES

functional attributes in the leader as servant leadership, but they can share some overlapping functions with the outbound attributes.

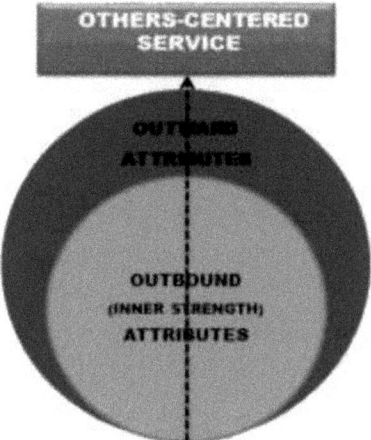

Figure 1.1. Servant leadership functional attributes

In summary, a leadership attribute is more than an ability or a characteristic; it is making those characteristics or abilities functional as part of how the leader acts (his habits) in service to others and applying those characteristics (beyond just having them) in personal and service relations to others. The character or known characteristic defines some aspects of your abilities or who you are inside— e.g. honest, humble, brave, etc. Your attribute, on the other hand, defines your habits; a display of how you use your characteristics, or the actions you exhibit toward others because of who you are inside. For example, empathy as a leadership characteristic becomes a leadership attribute if the followers can distinguish the leader's acts or habits of empathy, such as walking through with his followers in their state of suffering to bring wholeness; otherwise, it is just a characteristic or ability. Leadership attributes toward others are what impact the followers' and the organizational growth more than ability and competence.

In addressing one of the self-righteous hypocritical attributes of servitude leadership, Jesus called leader-servants to be "inside-out" leaders that reflect credibility; indeed, leaders should not appear outwardly righteous when they are full of hypocrisy and lawlessness in their hearts. He was describing "inside–out" as an authentic leadership attribute measured by the display of credibility a leadership attribute!

ALS Responsibility Leadership Attributes, Principles, & Practices

The measuring stick of a leader-servant is Jesus Christ. We measure ourselves unto the measure of the status of the fullness of Christ (Ephesians 4:13).

The leadership attributes of an authentic leader as a servant are encapsulated in **SERVANT/SERVING LEADERSHIP** are listed in Table 1.1, and defined in Table 1.2: *Servanthood, Emulation, Responsibility, Vision, Navigation, Adaptability, Trust, Listening, Empathy, Affection, Discipleship, Encouragement, Reproduction, Stewardship, Healing-Care, Initiation, Integrity,* and *Persuasion*. Other support attributes include *Influence, Courage, and Generosity*.

The attributes have been separated into Outward and Outbound (Inner Strength) leadership Attributes. As shown in Table 1.1, each of these attributes has three or more leadership characteristics. As such, more than 65 leadership characteristics are covered in these 20 attributes. For example, a leader's Servanthood leadership attribute is characterized by his willing servant's heart of selfless role humility, sacrifice, and submissiveness. The more these are present in a leader, the more effective the servant leadership.

Table 1.1: The functional leader-servant leadership Outbound (Inner Strength) and Outward attributes

	LEADER-SERVANT LEADERSHIP ATTRIBUTES			INNER STRENGTH ATTRIBUTES	OUTWARD ATTRIBUTES
S	Servanthood	L	Listening	Adaptability	Affection
E	Emulation	E	Empathy	Courage	Discipleship
R	Responsibility	A	Affection	Empathy	Emulation
V	Vision	D	Discipleship	Encouragement	Generosity
A	Adaptability	E	Encouragement	Initiation	Healing–Care
N	Navigation	R	Reproduction	Listening	Influence
T	Trust	S	Stewardship	Navigation	Persuasion
I	Influence	H	Healing–Care	Responsibility	Reproduction
G	Generosity	I	Initiation	Stewardship	Servanthood
C	Courage	P	Persuasion	Vision	Trust/Integrity

The list does not assume that a leader has to be excellent in all attributes or even have all of them to be an effective Leader–Servant. However, the more of these attributes the leader displays in his acts of

CHAPTER 1
UNDERSTANDING LEADERSHIP ATTRIBUTES

service toward others, the more productive he or she will be, and the further his impact on the followers and organization. The table also shows that two or more attributes can share common characteristics, which can be applied or observed in different contexts. For example, a leader's ability to inspire followers can be seen in his acts of discipleship, empowerment, an.d encouragement attributes in the context in which these attributes apply. Each attribute is exhibited either as a part of the outbound inner strength attribute of a leader or a part of the outward attribute. Table 1.1 is not an exhaustive list of attributes; in fact, there are hundreds of such attributes. This is just the starting point.

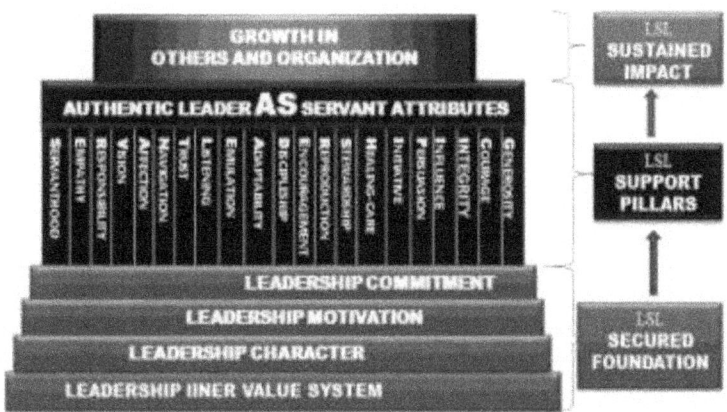

Figure 1.2: Servant leadership outward attributes (dark blue) and relationship to four foundational layers of the LSL Model

Figure 1.2 shows that the leader's attributes are shaped and secured by his four foundational layers (leadership inner value system, leadership character, motivation, and commitment). The attributes of the leader–servants are also conceptualized as the support pillars that will establish and support the personal authenticity of the leader, what the leader, does and the effectiveness of the leadership process. Thus, the attributes represent functional pillars of authentic leadership that can be learned or enriched as described in detail in the subsequent chapters. The combined effect of a secured foundation and stable support pillars will make a sustained impact on the growth of followers and the organization.

COMPARISONS WITH OTHER WORKS

The original works by Greenleaf (1970) in servant leadership [1] have been reviewed by Larry Spears (1996), who identified listening, empathy, healing, awareness, persuasion, conceptualization, foresight, stewardship, commitment to the growth of others, and building community as the ten distinguishing characteristics of servant leadership. [2] Russell (2001) has studied these attributes and have shown them to be essential in servant leadership and concluded that these qualities generally "grow out of the inner values and beliefs of individual leaders." [3] Russell and Stone (2002) extended the Greenleaf 10 attributes to 20 attributes observed in servant-leaders. These 20 attributes were categorized by these authors as either functional attributes (intrinsic characteristics of servant-leaders) or accompanying attributes (complement attributes that enhance the functional attributes).[4] The operational attributes were identified as vision, honesty, integrity, trust, modeling, service, pioneering, appreciation, and empowerment with the accompanying attributes of communication, credibility, competence, stewardship, visibility, influence, persuasion, listening, encouragement, teaching, and delegation. Only three of the attributes identified by Greenleaf were identified, and all three were accompanying attributes rather than functional. Responsibility, adaptability, affection, discipleship, navigation, and reproduction attributes which are considered critical in biblical-based servant leadership in my LSL model are not covered by Russell and Greenleaf. As shown in the description of the attributes in Table 1.2, most of the attributes reported by Russell and Stone (2002)[5] or Greenleaf [1] can be seen either in the twenty attributes or their associated characteristics. Integrity and honesty for example are leadership characteristics of trust and other attributes rather than an independent attributes. I take the position that servant leadership attributes are functional attributes in acts of duty to others and emanate from the inner value system of the leader.

CHAPTER 1
UNDERSTANDING LEADERSHIP ATTRIBUTES

Table 1.2: Description of the functional leader-servant outward leadership attributes and associated principles and characteristics

Leader–Servant Leadership Attributes	Principles of Leadership Attributes	Leadership Characteristics
Affection: *This is the combined love-based works toward providing the essential help or services for the spiritual growth or survival of another person. .* (Chapter 2)	*Affection flows from a person to produce positive emotions for the well-being of another person*	Kindness Compassion Practical Love Affective signs Appreciation
Discipleship: *This is the combined acts of personally developing, intentionally equipping, and attentively empowering growth in others to reproduce a heart of service.* (Chapter 3)	*Discipleship transforms and empowers followers for service leadership that grows communities.*	Inspiring Shepherding Equipping Developing Empowering
Emulation: *This is the combined acts of initiating an authentic servant attitude as a model of service worthy of following* (Chapter 4)	*A great leader-servant outwardly and positively inspires a pattern of good works for others to follow.*	Inspiration Motivation Initiation Model Following
Generosity: *This is the combined acts of freely sharing with and giving to others as an act of kindness, without expectation of reward or return to him.* (Chapter 5)	*Generosity is an outward measure of the level of sacrifice, what is shared, or the impact a giving makes, not just the size of the giving.*	Sharing Giving Kindness Affection Love
Healing-Care: *This is the combined acts of providing comfort and empathy to make others whole emotionally and spiritually along with tending to the follower's physical and mental well-being.* (Chapter 6)	*Comforting others in any trouble with the comfort with which we are comforted by God, brings healing - wholeness.*	Self-Healing Empathy Reconciliation Comfort Relational
Influence: *This is the combined acts of positively affecting desired change in conduct,*	*The true measure of leadership success in affecting*	Model Positive attitude Authority

performance, and relational connections toward others-centered course of action or service. (Chapter 7)	desired change in conduct, performance, and relational connections in others is influence	Connection Wisdom Intelligence,
Persuasion: This is the combined acts of communicating perspective to connect, challenge, and convince with a compelling purpose to convert others to a new position. (Chapter 8)	The means of transforming others to a new perspective is through empathetic persuasion	Connecting Challenging Communicating Convincing Converting Encouraging
Reproduction: This is the combined acts of developing your leadership qualities in others and releasing them as successors to continue a greater mission. (Chapter 9)	Great leaders produce successors for legacy and greater courses as an expected product of an effective leadership reproduction.	Selecting Mentoring Equipping Empowering Releasing
Servanthood: This is the combined acts of humility, willingness, and intentionality in service to others through selfless sacrifice and submission as a servant. (Chapter 10)	A leader-servant is most qualified to lead when most ready to serve as a servant for the growth of others. The role of a leader is to serve as a servant	Servant's heart Humility Sacrifice Service Willingness Submissiveness
Trust: This is the combined acts of positive display of character, competence, credibility, and shared relational connections that produce assured trust-confidence of the trustee in the trusted. (Chapter 11)	True leadership trust produces assured trustee's confidence and readiness to follow based on the credibility, competence, and shared relational connections of the trusted.	Character Competence Integrity Credibility Confidence

PRINCIPLE OF LEADERSHIP ATTRIBUTE

In the context of servant leadership, a leadership attribute is a level above the leadership characteristic or trait of a leader. The principle of leadership attribute states that every leadership attribute has a set of distinguishing characteristics that make up the inward or outward display of the attribute. The principle reflects the essential designed purpose or outcome of the attribute or the inevitable consequence of the effective practice of the attribute. Thus, the principle of leadership attribute is a concise statement about the fundamental truth, value, or belief about the attribute in a leadership situation; it is a statement that establishes an idea about the outcome of the attribute for guiding the practical application of the attribute and its characteristics. I will postulate and frame each principle as an additive function of the characteristics of the attribute. A statement of each principle is quoted at the beginning or below the title of each chapter. It is yet to be experimentally proven if the attribute is a linear or some other non-linear function of these characteristics as variables. It is expected, however, that each character will contribute to the effectiveness of the attribute in varying degrees.

AUTHENTIC LEADERSHIP ATTRIBUTES

At a personal level, attributes are the value-based inside-out moral leadership assets that can be related to the authenticity of a leader-servant. The complexity of defining authenticity has been noted in the literature. The subject of authentic leadership is well covered in the works of Terry (1993),[5] George (2003),[6] and Shair and Eilam (2005).[7] All appear to agree that authenticity requires self-awareness and objective self-identity in personal and social interactions with others. In his book, *Advocacy Leadership*, Professor Gary L. Anderson offers individual, organizational, and societal perspectives on authenticity: "Authenticity, at a peculiar level, is living a life, whether in the private or professional term. This is congruent with one's espoused values; at the structural level, authenticity has to do with viewing human beings as ends in themselves, rather than means to other ends; at the public level, it is a state of affairs that is congruous with the shared political and cultural values of society."[8]

The basic tenets of these perspectives are very fitting to authenticity as a qualifying element of leader-servant leadership attributes. The attribute reflects how the followers see the leader based on the leader's distinctive features displayed through his or her actions personally, organizationally, and societally. The leader is seen as a leader-servant or serving leader because the followers see him lead as a servant from an inside-out value of others. This is what makes the leader authentic.

Authenticity means that what a leader displays outside, in personal or leadership life of service to others, and society is based on the values the leader espouses inside.

Authenticity in servant leadership can be one or two types or both: *Outbound Authenticity and Outward Authenticity*: The Outbound (outward-bound) Authenticity is the genuineness of personal honesty from your inner strength and abilities; what you say and how you act emanate from who you are or how you feel inside. It reflects the essential truth and honesty about your outward-bound inner strength.

Outward authenticity, on the other hand, describes the truthfulness of your credibility and honesty displayed outward in relation to others; your *outer* visible behavior or how you act outwardly towards others reflects exactly your true intentions.

While *outward* authenticity is the visible *outer* indicator of the truth of who you are inside, *outbound* authenticity is outward-bound attribute from the inside of who you are. Credibility in this context is the influence a leader has to attract believability, trustworthiness, and authenticity; it is the believability, trustworthiness, and authenticity of who you are inside and outside.

A key element of personal authenticity is that it is seen or measured in the context of societal, cultural, and organizational interactions. In that context, achieving individual authenticity becomes a challenge since it is influenced by social factors and dispositions of individuals who usually depend on liberal and organizational realities. However, for leader-servant leadership, the leader can face those changing times by remaining focused on his key Biblical-based principles or *Leadership Inner Value System*. Thus, I am interested in authenticity as an essential element of effective Leader-servant leadership attributes or Leader-servant leadership attributes as drivers of leadership authenticity. With that in mind, the first critical element of authenticity in practicing or developing efficient leader-servant leadership attributes is inside-out self-examination relative to the people served rather than the organization. You may ask yourself: What will be my response when the people I lead act or react in a certain way, will it be negative or positive? What are my strengths and vulnerabilities at those times?

Professor Yacobi in his post, "Elements of Human Authenticity," noted that since "the self -arise attribute emerges from interactions between self, others, and the environment in a complex society and world, there may co-exist multiple complicated identities depending on place and context." [9] He went on to identify the following <u>essential elements of personal authenticity</u>: self-awareness, unbiased self-examination, accurate self-knowledge, reflective judgment, personal responsibility, and integrity, genuineness, and humility, empathy for others, understanding of others, optimal utilization of feedback from others. All of these are covered under the leadership attributes or characteristics shown in Table 1.2.

Bill George, in his book, *Authentic Leadership*, takes the position that to be an authentic leader; a person must have the following essential characteristics: [10]

- Behavior based on value: He must understand his own values and exhibit behavior to others based on those values;
- He must not compromise his values in difficult situations but could use the situation to strengthen personal values in those situations.
- Passion from a clear purpose: Be self-aware of who he is, where he is going, and the right thing to do.
- Compassion from the heart: He must lead from a compassionate heart that allows them to be sensitive to the plight and needs of others,
- Connectedness from a relationship; he must be relationally connected with people he leads,
- Consistency from the self-disciple: He must demonstrate self-discipline to remain calm, collected, and consistent in a stressful situation.

Modeled after the elements above, Table 1.3 lists six essential characteristics of authenticity for servant leadership. These fundamental characteristics cover the five identified above and can also be aligned with the leadership characteristics in Table 1.2. Each attribute in Table 1.2 is expected to pass the personal authenticity test in Tables 1.3, 1.4. In a survey of 132 Christian leaders, seventy-four percent (74%) of them agreed that they always or frequently exhibit servant leadership attributes. [11] Thus, a pass of the outward authenticity test means that a pure leader must demonstrate 70% or more of these essential elements of this legitimacy. (That is, 70% YES in the assessment questions in Tables 1.3, 1.4).

It needs to be noted, however, that a secular leader could be authentic and still lack some of the essential servant leadership attributes or characteristics such as selflessness, servanthood, and love-motivated servant attitudes of a leader-servant. Effective leader-servants are authentic leaders and personal authenticity is an essential element of leader-servant leadership. The key test for leader-servant authenticity is the quality of his inside-out value and personal character. What is most important is a change from the inside-out.

Table 1.3: The test of essential elements of personal inner strength authenticity in servant leadership

	Elements of Inner Strength Authenticity	Inner Strength (Outbound) Authenticity Assessment Questions	YES / NO
1	Personal inside-out value-based behavior	Are your personal inside-out values aligned with acts of service and behavior outside?	1
		Are you honest to yourself in relation to your inner strengths and abilities?	2
2	Inside-out Self-Awareness	Do you have unbiased self-examination, and accurate self-knowledge of who you are inside-out?	3
		Do you know your inner strength and weaknesses in relation to the good you want to show as an outward attribute?	4
3	Inside-out Empathy-Compassion	Do you know and feel from your inside what you want for your followers?	5
		Are you motivated to empathize, based on your inside feelings?	6
4	Inside-out Connection with followers	Do you feel deep, personal, and spiritual connection with your followers?	7
		Does what you say and how you act reflect how you feel when you relate to others?	8
5	Inside-out Emotional Self-regulation	Do you have difficulty controlling your emotion in order to remain calm in a stressful situation?	9
		Are you always able to comfort yourself?	10
6	Inside-out Authenticity Feedback	Do your followers see your inside-out value from your outside behavior?	11
		Will your followers feel that what you say you are is congruent with how you act?	12
#YESs_____; # NOs_____: Outbound Authenticity: YES/ 12-----%			

CHAPTER 1
UNDERSTANDING LEADERSHIP ATTRIBUTES

Table 1.4: The test of essential elements of personal outward authenticity in servant leadership

	Elements of Personal Outward Authenticity	Personal Outward Authenticity Assessment Questions	YES or NO
1	Personal value-based outward behavior	Are your personal values and beliefs aligned with your acts of service and behavior toward others?	1
		Do you live out your life according to your beliefs?	2
2	Personal Self-Awareness	Do you have clarity of your personal vision and purpose?	3
		Does what you know about yourself accurately describe what others say?	4
3	Personal Outward Empathy-Compassion	Do you apply how you feel to what your followers need?	5
		Do you lead from a compassionate heart and are you sensitive to the plight and needs of others?	6
4	Personal Connection with followers	Do you feel deep, personal connection with your followers?	7
		Does your outward action toward others reflect exactly your true intentions?	8
5	Outward Emotional Self-regulation	Do you have difficulty controlling your emotions to remain calm in a stressful situation?	9
		Does your evaluation of your value of others agree with how valued they feel?	10
6	Personal Authenticity Feedback	Do your followers see your outward acts as true and honest?	11
		Can your followers see other-centeredness in 70% or more of your attributes?	12
#YESs____; # NOs____: Outbound Authenticity: YES/ 12-----%			

SUMMARY 1
UNDERSTANDING LEADERSHIP PROCESS

Before starting this exercise, please read and follow the instruction in the preface of this workbook. Answers to these questions are contained in this chapter. Completion of these exercises after reading the chapter should take 60-90 minutes.

Discovering the Leadership Attributes

1. What is your alternative definition of leadership? In learning to lead, how would you differentiate the following elements:
    a. Leadership.
    b. Leader as servant leadership.
    c. Leadership characteristics.
    d. Leadership attributes.
2. What are the key differences between the Leader as Servant and the Servant as Leader Leadership philosophies?
3. What was the original source of the Servant as Leader (SL)? What was the original source of Leader as Servant (LS)?
4. What is the key framework of a Leader as a Servant Leadership?
5. Authenticity in servant leadership can be one or two types or both *Outbound Authenticity and Outward Authenticity*: Describe a time when you displayed:
    a. The Outbound (outward-bound)—*outbound* authenticity is outward-bound attribute from the inside of who you are.
    b. *The Outward Authenticity*—*outward* authenticity is the visible *outer* indicator of the truth of who you are inside,
6. Describe the key elements of personal authenticity seen or measured in the context of societal, cultural, and organizational interactions.
7. How are the essential characteristics of authentic leader in leadership process in challenging times?
8. How much of a leader-servant are you? Take the personal leader-servant audit in Table 1.5 to self-assess your effectiveness.
9. Based on the questions in Table 1.5, can you identify each of the twenty attributes? What ones did you score 3 ("sometimes") or less than 3? Review and learn and commit to work to improve.

CHAPTER 1
UNDERSTANDING LEADERSHIP ATTRIBUTES

Table 1.5. Leader As Servant-Leadership Audit

A servant-leader in his leadership position purposefully choses to serve and inspire acts of service in others by his example. Select and circle best answer to questions
1=Never: 2=Almost never ; 3=Sometimes; 4=Frequently; 5 =Always

	Servant Leadership assessment questions	Circle no
1	I am willing and other-centered, and readily chose to serve others as a servant for their personal growth	1 2 3 4 5
2	I model others-centered attitude in my service and relationships and inspire same for others to follow	1 2 3 4 5
3	I have a sense of obligation, willingness, and accountability for the service towards others	1 2 3 4 5
4	I have the foresightedness to specify in the present view what others' growth should be in a given future	1 2 3 4 5
5	I work toward providing the essential help or services for the spiritual growth or survival of the others;	1 2 3 4 5
6	I provide the needed purposeful course of action for how to chart the course to for my followers.	1 2 3 4 5
7	I display external credibility and a strong sense of character based on values, beliefs, and competence;	1 2 3 4 5
8	In communication, I attentively perceive and hear what is communicated, reflectively listen to understand and to be understood	1 2 3 4 5
9	I walk through with others in their state (suffering, emotions, etc.) in a way that provides the needed care and well-being	1 2 3 4 5
10	I have a measure of self-secured flexibility to adapt appropriate attitude to serve all people in different situations	1 2 3 4 5
11	I personally develop, intentionally equip, and attentively nurture spiritually growth in others	1 2 3 4 5
12	My act of bravery instills in others the courage and confidence to follow or persevere in a course of action	1 2 3 4 5
13	I develop my leadership qualities in others as successors to continue in a purposeful mission	1 2 3 4 5
14	I manage , maintain,, and account for all resources entrusted to me and being responsible for the difference my acts make	1 2 3 4 5
15	As a care-giver, I act to comfort and make others whole emotionally	1 2 3 4 5
16	When I see a need, I originate a vision and action, and stay committed to meet that need and desired change	1 2 3 4 5

ALS RESPONSIBILITY LEADERSHIP
ATTRIBUTES, PRINCIPLES, & PRACTICES

17	I display a holistic view of an issue to inform, transform or convert others to my view through empathetic persuasion	1	2	3	4	5
18	I freely share what I have sacrificially as an act of kindness to others, without expectation of reward in return	1	2	3	4	5
19	My act of influence is to affect the actions, behavior, opinions, etc., of others based on trust, credibility and relationship	1	2	3	4	5
20	In the face challenges and danger, I act with bravery to overcome fear and take a stand with strength and conviction	1	2	3	4	5
Score Range	Add up the numbers in each column Check and Understand the key areas to work on					
81-100	Strong Leader-Servant; keep it up, go and train others.	Total _____				
66-80	Above average Leader-Servant; work 25% of key areas					
50-65	Average but developing; need to work on 50% of key areas					
34-49	Below average leader; work on 75% of key areas					
<34	Not a Leader-Servant; need training in all areas					

CHAPTER 2
RESPONSIBILITY LEADERSHIP ATTRIBUTE

Leadership responsibility is the measure of the quality of a Leader's accountability for the growth of followers and the organization

An element of responsibility is always associated with effective leadership as clearly shown in the literature. Responsibility itself is normally characterized by two elements: *Accountability*, being answerable for the outcome of performance), and freedom of action to meet an *obligation* at work, as in being responsible for the assigned duty or obligation. According to Cameron and Caza in this context, responsibility means "response-able, or possessing the capability and the accountability needed to respond." [13] As indicated above, responsibility and accountability are the dualism at the core of any leadership for it defines the position in a leadership continuum. At a personal level, it defines the level of your position (pastor, deacon, department head, janitor, etc.) in your church, family, or employment. Are there qualities in that position for which you have been called, chosen, or mandated? Is there anyone else that can perform your duties? Can you teach another person how to be in your position or can you model it? Or can you delegate it or give it away? What is the consequence of not taking responsibility? Organizationally, what are the attributes of the leadership structure, process, and culture that are most conducive for maximizing the growth of followers and organizations in service toward others? What are the dominant characteristics of those attributes, and how can they be developed to enhance high-quality relationships, emotional competencies, positive communication, beneficial energy development, and positive climates for the effective leader as a servant leadership process?

Responsibility attribute is a critical attribute of servant leadership. This chapter explores Responsibility as an attribute of the leader-servant as he or she serves others. I will attempt to answer these questions by exploring the distinguishing leadership characteristics of responsibility attributes. Functional definition and principle of responsibility attribute will be framed based on those characteristics.

CHARACTERISTICS OF RESPONSIBILITY ATTRIBUTE

What differentiates the office of the president from the secretary, or the office of the Pastor from the deacons, and so on, is the responsibility incumbent on the person or the office? The office defines the obligation, but it is the leader that is accountable for what the office does and how he enables the dynamics of what makes up the office. In that sense, there is a third dimension of responsibility very relevant to the responsibility attribute in servant leadership. It is the enablement of the appropriate desired outcome. This covers a leader's *willingness* or inclination to act appropriately or enable appropriate action in his followers or organization. Appropriateness in this sense associates' responsible action with what is right, correct, or beneficial. Behaving responsibly means doing well or doing what is appropriate in a given situation. [55] This third dimension is the least emphasized in secular leadership compared to the other two—accountability or obligation—and yet the most critical in producing the desired outcome in servant leadership.

Loosely speaking, responsibility is the act of being responsible (trustworthy, dependable, honest, etc.). Thus, this attribute is displayed in the process of leading followers or an organization in such a way that it can be referred to as responsible leadership. Responsible leadership emphasizes an affirmative orientation toward the enablement of positive human capability; it focuses on influencing positive outcomes in people and organizations and the processes that produce those outcomes. Cameron and Caza (2005), in their comprehensive, article, "Developing strategies for responsible leadership," [13] a theory laid the essential foundation that will help identify the characteristics of leadership responsibility attribute in the organization, and the key elements of *willingness* as the third dimension of responsibility attribute. Responsible leaders, according to these authors, "are unusual in that they *choose* to emphasize the positive, uplifting, and flourishing side of organizational life" rather than the negative. This definition is important in reference to the idea of "unusual" intentional choosing in the context of a leader as a servant leadership mindset. The strategies those responsible leaders (that is, those displaying responsibility attributes) can use to enable and enhance positive outcomes include: *positive climate, positive calling orientation, positive connections,* and *positive communication.*[13]

Positive climate: Climate refers to individuals' psychological experiences associated with the work environment. [13,14] This means, that a positive climate is one in which positive feelings and interpretations are the predominant feeling more than negative feelings and interpretations. Citing several studies by Fredrickson, [15, 16] Cameron, and Casa concluded that "positive climate leads to positive emotions which, in turn, lead to optimal individual and organizational functioning" [13]; it also creates a positive work climate that enhances decision making, productivity, creativity, social integration, and pro-social behaviors. [17] Other studies [18] confirmed that inducing positive emotion ns enlarges cognitive perspectives, which enhance the individual's ability to attend to more information, make richer interpretations, and experience higher levels of creativity and productivity.

Positive Connections: These are those connections that function together to enhance relationships between individuals and between individuals and the organization. It includes such things as friendships, compassion, forgiveness, and gratitude in the organization through the processes of collective noticing, collective feeling, and collective responding. [19] The presence of positive and supportive relationships was shown to have positive effects on individuals and subsequently on their performance—as well as on their collective performance in an organization—because of their association with very basic physiological processes.

Positive Communication: Positive communication occurs in an organization when affirmative and supportive language replaces negative and critical language. According to Cameron and Caza (2005), in reviewing key studies on the subject, "the single most important factor in predicting team performance—which was more than twice as powerful as any other factor—was the ratio of positive comments to negative comments." [13] Positive comments are those that express appreciation, support, helpfulness, or compliments. Negative comments express criticism, disapproval, or blame.

Positive Calling Orientation: An important factor in servant leadership as referenced in the Scriptures is the concept of one's calling or mission in life. Several studies have pointed out that individuals typically hold one of three broad orientations toward work: work as a *job*, as a *career*, or as a *calling*. [20] As should be expected, those who see work as a *job*, do so primarily for the financial or material rewards it provides, seeking no particular personal satisfaction from their work; individuals with a *career* orientation are motivated primarily by the success, and work toward achieving the prestige, power, recognition, and advancement from performing their work well; and those with the sense of work as a calling works for the sake and meaningfulness of the work itself, and considers work as a mission inherently fulfilling; they selflessly seek for a greater good from the work, regardless of personal reward. This orientation yields more positive outcomes and superior individual and organizational performance than other orientations. "Workers with a calling orientation reported higher job and life satisfaction scores compared to those with career or job orientations, as well as high satisfaction with their organization and their work." [13]

We can conclude from the above review that a leader is responsible for what he is *obligated* to and *committed to*. If the leader's *willingness* and *enablement for* appropriate desired outcomes are missing, the obligation will not be met; if accountability is missing, but all other qualities are present, the leader will lose focus on the outcomes of his responsibility. For example, if a shepherd of a flock of sheep has a sense of obligation and willingness to feed the sheep but has no sense of *accountability*, he will not notice when one of the sheep is missing; indeed, he cannot, therefore, feel responsible for the loss. In contrast, a leader's sense of accountability is a measure of his or her ultimate sense of responsibility. As we learned in the Parable of the Lost Sheep, (Luke 15:3-7) when a shepherd feels accountable, he feels responsible, he will search out the lost sheep and will rejoice when he finds it.

Yes, responsibility can be learned or assigned, but once it is assigned the leader becomes accountable and cannot delegate the responsibility for the task to someone else. If the responsibility to lead is missing in a leader, followers take ownership of the duty based on their senses of what is needed. The result is often confusion and stagnation or the organization loses unity of purpose. John C. Maxwell, in his book, *'Talent is Never Enough'* discussed the following four ways that responsibility can strengthen a leader's talents: [21]

1. Responsibility provides the *foundation* of success.
2. Responsibility handled correctly, leads to more responsibility. These additional responsibilities and the ability to do well in them lead to an *expansion* of the use of one's talents and provide opportunities for growth and promotion.
3. Responsibility *maximizes ability* and opportunity because it causes people to take actions that produce results.
4. Responsibility over time builds a *solid reputation*. A leader's ability to take responsibility *creates trust* from others and casts the leader as dependable.

The above provisions of responsibility play key roles in secular, non-secular, and corporate worlds. How do you compare the different leadership roles of individuals in a team working toward one goal? We can see this illustrated in the game of American football. I am not a typical fan of American football; in fact, I have only attended one game in 34 years. I still do not even understand why we call it "football" but play the game, mainly with hands. However, one particular homecoming game was special as we sat together in a comfortable reserved game box with members of the Board of Visitors and some University trustees. I appreciated the honor of sitting with these movers and shakers from their different corporations and viewed it as an opportunity to network and build relationships before the board meeting scheduled for the next day. I could not help but compare the leadership roles these individuals assumed with the game of football and the responsibilities, the quarterback and each member of the team took on in their assigned, obligated responsibilities to the team.

As the quarterback carried the ball, I was thinking about the awesome responsibility he had to receive the ball, carry the ball, and throw or pass it accurately before being "sacked." At the other end, was the running back or the receiver who had to catch the ball and sprint for the touchdown! Each individual on the team had one thing in common: they were responsible for winning and for each other. Each member shared the responsibility for what happened to the ball, to the team, to the club or university, and the fans, those in the stadium, and all those all over the world watching and cheering.

As they each carried the ball or waited to carry the ball, each player must guard against slipping and mistakes, be ready to recover from a fumble, and at the same time, care for each other. Each must have a sense of obligation and the willingness to meet that obligation voluntarily. They must all be ready to account for what happens to that ball and their teammates.

Turning my attention to all the distinguished executives in the room, I wondered how these top leaders were carrying the ball in their respective roles. They also had one responsibility in common: they worked to make their companies great, and their success depended very much on their leadership responsibility attribute.

What would a successful company look like if the leaders were a responsible team like a football team? Are secular or corporate leaders and their employees always accountable or feel obligated to take care of their teammates (employees)? What does winning really mean to these leaders? I post that winning means productivity and results. A leader's strong sense of accountability creates an organizational culture of responsibility and accountability to win; that is, to achieve the desired result. A culture of accountability fosters an opportunity for people to become engaged as part of the team for a solution. Nevertheless, it is most effective when people see accountability in the leaders who model accountability through their behavior, attitude, actions, and reactions. Such modeling starts with leaders assuming full responsibility for their thoughts, feelings, actions, and results. When leaders assume full responsibility, they show accountability and acquire the moral capital and ability to influence desired outcomes in others' sense of responsibility. A culture of accountability sustains productivity and achievement as a trickle-down game-changer. Robert Slater, the author of 29 *Leadership Secrets from Jack Welch* cited one of

Jack Welch's leadership secrets: "By making your employees more accountable, you make your organization more productive." [12] As one of the leading authorities in this subject of leadership, Jack Welch's work is well recognized and has made marks in many organizations.

Another effect of accountability of leaders working as a team is to increase the responsiveness of the organization to the needs of internal employees and external customers; leading to better performance metrics, products, and a sense of meaningfulness and impact. Better job performance means greater rewards and therefore, better job satisfaction. Everybody wins!

OnPoint Consulting conducted a survey of 400 leaders of top-performing companies and identified five actions that have the greatest impact on an organization's ability to build a culture of accountability and achieve more results: [22]

1. **Translate strategy into specific objectives.** This involves clarifying priorities and translating these into specific departmental goals. This leads to clearer department goals by facilitating goal-setting at the individual level which enhances accountability at all levels. This also increases the likelihood that implementation plans will be targeted toward high-impact outcomes.
2. **Coordinate actions across levels and work units.** This is a follow-up on progress as a critical aspect of execution essential for building a culture of accountability and keeping people focused on high-priority goals and actions. Accountability requires leaders to monitor goals and reinforce appropriate actions and behaviors.
3. **Provide accurate and timely information to employees.** This strategy involves clear communication about priorities, as well as an ongoing dialogue between managers and their direct reports. Goal setting and coaching are key elements of most organizations' performance management systems and important tools to drive growth and desired results.
4. **Ensure that your actions are consistent with company objectives, values, and priorities.** To expect people to be accountable, leaders must model and display a positive attitude toward accountability and must be responsive when people fail

to be responsible. Otherwise, those who work toward accountability will feel the leader is not serious about his expectation. If employees are not held accountable when they fail in their responsibilities, leaders will be weakened in their effort to push for the expectations of others. Followers will trust or not follow a leader who is not living up to the same expectation and values he requires of others.

5. **Clarify expectations and head off potential problems**. This means clarifying exactly what the priorities are and what needs to be done, establishing a specific date of completion of the task, and agreeing on performance metrics to review progress.

PRINCIPLE OF LEADERSHIP RESPONSIBILITY ATTRIBUTE

The above introduction is intentionally long compared to others because of its importance in the overall list of attributes being discussed. However, we can conclude that responsibility-attribute reflects the leader's sense of obligation to carry out the duties of his position willingly. A responsible leader-servant feels personally accountable to his followers and the impact and outcomes of his actions on both his followers and the organization. Thus, the primary distinguishing leadership characteristics of responsibility attribute can be summarized as *Obligation or Commitment, Willingness, and Accountability*. With respect to servant leadership, here is my functional definition:

> *Servant leadership responsibility attribute is a leader's combined acts of meeting an obligation and willingness to account for the service entrusted to him to impact others internally and externally positively.*

Although meeting an obligation is one of the characteristics of responsibility; to be responsible is more than just meeting an obligation. One can have the ability to meet an obligation and yet not be responsible or have a responsibility as an attribute; accountability is the measure of meeting an obligation. We posit the following servant leadership responsibility principle:

CHAPTER 2
RESPONSIBILITY LEADERSHIP ATTRIBUTE

Servant leadership responsibility principle: The responsibility is the measure of the quality of a leader's accountability for the growth of followers and the organization.

A leader's action to meet an obligation—growth of followers and organization— reach the level of measure of responsibility as an attribute only if that act is accompanied by a deep sense of commitment and willingness to be accountable for actions taken. Thus, the principle is reframed as: Responsibility is a quality of accountability to an obligation and can be expressed as:

OBLIGATION + WILLINGNESS + ACCOUNTABILITY = RESPONSIBILITY

The above equation means that the responsibility of a leader-servant is his ability to act on his willingness diligently and to meet positional obligations while also remaining personally accountable to his followers and for the outcomes of his actions. As modeled in Figure 10, a leader's sense of obligation drives his or her willingness to meet the obligation and his readiness to be accountable for the outcomes is based on his willingness.

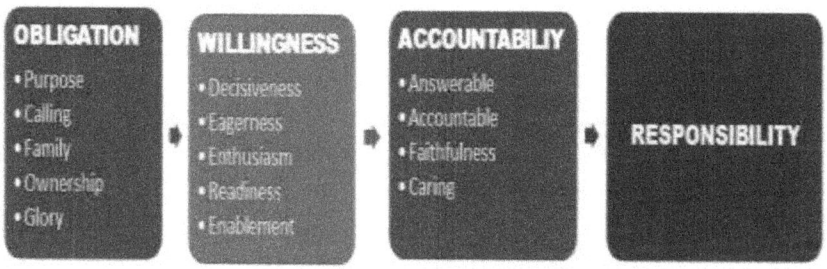

Figure 10: Three-stage progression model of leadership responsibility attribute

The model shows a progression of sequential steps that starts with a clear understanding of the expectation and purpose to which the leader is obligated, followed by his willingness to commit to meeting the duty trust requirements. The process ends with a readiness and sense of accountability for the outcomes.

SUMMARY 2
DEVELOPING RESPONSIBILITY LEADERSHIP ATTRIBUTE

Discovering Responsibility Leadership Attribute

1. What are the dominant characteristics of responsibility leadership attribute
2. What would you consider the three distinguishing characteristics of the responsibility leadership attribute?
3. What is the consequence of not taking responsibility?
4. How does responsibility differentiate the office of the leader?
5. State the Principle of Leadership Responsibility Attribute
6. With respect to servant leadership, frame a functional definition of *Servant leadership responsibility attribute*
7. State the additive law of Responsibility leadership attribute

Practicing the Acts of Responsibility-Attribute

1. What are your five inclinations to decisiveness to Act or ways to overcome indecision?
2. Responsibility-Accountability is defined as the sense of personal ownership or liability of the obligation in the leadership responsibility.
   a. How can a follower be accountable to the Leader?
   b. How can the same leader be accountable to the follower?
3. What are some eight strategic actions a follower and the leader needs to develop for positive attitude toward accountability?
4. How can the acts of responsibility be developed to enhance high-quality relationships and positive climates for the effective leader as a servant leadership process?
5. How many acts of responsibility as an attribute do you display?
6. Take the leadership responsibility attribute audit in Table AII.8. Which responsibility qualities or questions did you score < 3?
7. With reference to responsibility leadership attribute, what take-away, meaning or lesson can you frame to improve your acts of responsibility attribute in a leadership process?
8. Write a commitment statement for plan to improve.

CHAPTER 3
DEVELOPING RESPONSIBLITY-OBLIGATION

With respect to servant leadership, an obligation is a service or duty to which a leader has committed and to which he or she feels accountability to the followers and organization to perform successfully. Your obligation as a pastor of a church could be preaching the Word, counseling families, serving as the choir director, and leading the worship service. As a husband, your obligations could be to love and provide for your family. How can we determine the primary obligation of your calling in God's agenda? How can we meet the obligation? Whatever the obligations: they are binding relationships, and you are ultimately accountable for them. The obligation is part of your calling to God, and it needs to be met. Jesus said;

> *"I am the good shepherd. The good shepherd lays down his life for the sheep. The hired hand is not the shepherd and does not own the sheep. So when he sees the wolf coming, he abandons the sheep and runs away. Then, the wolf attacks the flock and scatters it" (John 10:11-12, NLT).*

In this scripture, Jesus demonstrated an example of obligation in responsibility as a leader-servant. Jesus identifies His obligation to the sheep; in fact, he puts the sheep before Himself. He Sacrifices himself if necessary. He values and protects the sheep. He knows the sheep, and the sheep know him. He compares this relationship to that of the "hired man" who does not feel any obligation, and, in the face of danger, *"The man runs away because he is a hired hand and cares nothing for the sheep" (John 10: 13, NLT).*

The Apostle Paul also modeled the answers on the issue of obligation in responsibility as shown in the following four obligation-responsible actions (1 Corinthians: 1:4-26; 2:1-5).

Understand and meet the purpose obligation.

The purpose-obligation involves knowing and accepting the purpose of the responsibility or the assigned duty. Paul wrote, "I always thank my God for you because of his grace given you in Christ Jesus. For in him, you have been enriched in every way. He will also keep you firm to the end so that you will be blameless on the day of our Lord Jesus Christ" (1 Corinthians 1:4-5, NIV). Understanding and meeting the purpose obligation involves understanding the reason and urgency for your call. To meet the purpose obligation, a leader must have the following senses:

Leaders and followers are in the purpose together by God's design and will. The leader and followers are called to and into a purpose to the church, the family, the employer, and so on. 'Paul called to be an apostle of Christ Jesus by the will of God…To the church of God in Corinth, to those sanctified in Christ Jesus and called to be his holy people, together" (1 Corinthians 1:1-2, NIV). The leader must recognize that to be called to the purpose involves taking ownership of the call as if it is the purpose of his very existence. To be called into the purpose means that he must have the sense that he was made to be part of the perfect will of God; that he is not only responsible for the call to meet the obligation, but he is part of the call. Jeremiah saw himself called and set aside for a purpose. He was on the call because he was part of the purpose. Nehemiah saw himself as part of the purpose of God to rebuild the broken walls of Jerusalem and its burned-down gates. He saw the need, captured the vision and purpose, and convinced the people that they were part of the purpose so that the people may "No longer be a reproach" (Nehemiah 1:4-2:8).

The leader and followers are part of destiny. The leader must understand that if the purpose obligation is missed, destiny will not be realized. This means that the leader will fail to complete the race or meet obligations if he loses the vision and purpose for the race. The 10 leaders sent with Joshua and Caleb to spy on the Promised Land completely missed the obligation purpose. They failed in their responsibilities as leaders and perished without reaching their covenant destiny in God. Sampson missed the sense of his calling, and he suffered and failed to finish strong. As a result, the people suffered. Jesus had a sense of His calling, even if it meant his death, and Paul answered his call and the responsibility to preach the gospel. A strong sense of destiny is like a bright light that keeps the leader's vision focused on the obligation purpose (Numbers 14:6-9).

Enable the positive orientation to your calling

Your calling is your purposeful mission related to your obligation identified above. The extent to which you effectively answer the call depends to a large extent on your sense of understanding the call as a selfless service to God. Your expected orientation is that your service toward others is for the sake and meaningfulness of the work itself and not for your reward. Thus, your sense of calling must be positive; that is, a sense that the work is an inherently fulfilling good mission beyond you and for a greater good, regardless of personal reward. Enabling positive calling orientation in yourself and your followers can be enhanced by enabling the identification of a sense of meaningfulness in obligated work. Positive calling orientation can be enabled by emphasizing the profound purpose, meaningfulness, and vision of abundance that triggers an intrinsic motivation in people. Research supports the connection between these enabling factors and a sense of calling at work. A sense of calling can be enhanced through at least four mechanisms identified in the literature. These include: [23]

(1) *Job enrichment* and *involvement,*
(2) *Intrinsic motivational factors,*
(3) *Empowering environment,* and
(4) Articulating a *clear vision of the future.*

A brief review of these is shown below:

Job enrichment and involvement- In his mechanism, *the* work is designed to provide enrichment through these five core job characteristics of skill variety, task identity, task significance, autonomy, and feedback as reasonably objective, measurable, and changeable properties of work for the desired psychological states of work, which in turn motivate positive personal/work outcomes. [24] Involvement includes direct and personal engagement, to enable personal growth. Work designed to provide personal growth and development opportunities has been shown to always be more meaningful than routine work.

The presence of intrinsic motivational factors- The factors addressed by this mechanism include interesting work, opportunities for creativity, chances for advancement and achievement, peer recognition, and personally fulfilling goals that are internally and inherently motivational according to Cameron and Caza (2005). [13] These factors enable the leader to see the impact of his calling passionately on the followers and for the followers to see their calling in the mission vision-mission defined by the leader.

Creating an empowering environment- An empowering environment is fully discussed elsewhere in this book and was shown to be a very effective enabling mechanism for growth in your calling, This mechanism provides opportunities to enable five essential dimensions of empowerment shown by research to be effective for both for individual performance and for organizational outcomes. These include: self-efficacy (a sense of competence), self-determination (a sense of choice), consequence (a sense of impact), meaningfulness (a sense of purpose), and trust (a sense of security).[25]

Articulating a clear vision of the future- This mechanism focuses on the vision that encourages and enables the highest potential in the followers. A clear vision focuses on abundance and opportunities, rather than on problems or obstacles. [26]

Understand and meet your family obligations.

Family obligation involves understanding for whom and in what "family" a leader is meeting obligations and the defining characteristics (good or bad) of a family or organization. Consider, for example: "I appeal to you, brothers and sisters, in the name of our Lord Jesus Christ, that all of you agree with one another in what you say and that there be no divisions among you, but that you be perfectly united in mind and thought… Is Christ divided?" (1 Corinthians 1:10-13, NIV). Understanding and meeting family obligations require us to have the following senses:

Members of the organization are perfectly joined together as one unit. The leader must lead the followers to recognize that members of the organization are perfectly joined together in the same mind and judgment. The act of meeting an obligation is important to the growth of a family. Any problems in the family are part of the leader's responsibility to solve. He takes no sides without placing one family against the other but treats all and judges all in the same way.

Consistently reminds the family of the purpose of the calling. To Paul, the purpose of his calling and his obligation was to preach the Gospel, and he consistently wrote to the churches to which he ministered to remind them of the purpose of his ministry and their respective obligations to each other in those churches. Jesus constantly reminded his disciples in many ways and the purpose of His calling. Leaders can remind followers of the purpose of the calling through service as exemplified by Paul and Jesus.

In most organizations, a common practice in which the leader engages at the beginning of the budget year is to circulate the organization's written vision, mission, and values. This document includes the responsibilities of each leader and the key performance indicators. A strategic plan is also another way of consistently updating the mission, goals, and objectives and communicating changes in the mission of the organization.

Everyone in the family will have different gifts and thus a distinctive impact. For a leader to meet family obligations or the needs of an individual member; he must have the sense that each member was created differently with different gifts of service. He must also understand that individuals were created for the same Lord, who does the "good work" in us as illustrated by the Apostle Paul in 1 Corinthians 12:5-6. The leader must facilitate the process and opportunities for the members to make the right choices to maximize their gifts.

Understand and meet ownership obligations.

Ownership obligation involves understanding, using President Truman's expression, that the "buck stops here." The leader is accountable for the success or failure of the organization for any specific call or duty. Understanding and meeting the ownership obligation requires us to have the following senses:

Have a sense of the responsibilities of success or failure. Understanding and admitting this and allowing followers to have the same sense is a critical first step in taking personal action to meet obligations and understanding what is needed to meet the obligation. A leader's attempt to blame others when things go wrong is usually to avoid taking responsibility.

Have a sense of responsibility for the team's success. This is one reason the leader is responsible for healing the followers. He must disciple them for growth and reproduce in them the qualities needed to be successful. If a leader fails to lead the followers on the right path, the followers will go astray, as sheep without a shepherd. They will drift away, and the leader shares the responsibility for the failure of the sheep.

The president of a particular organization once told me how dissatisfied he was with the performance of a member of his executive team in meeting obligations. "I am going to ask him to resign or the group to replace him," he said. This is a natural response of a secular power-control leader, who may be seeing this member as a threat to the group's success. This leader may see this reaction as passively avoiding confrontation or confrontation by eliminating the threat. To this leader, the failure is that of the executive team member, who did not do the job.

Sometimes followers will be slow to act, or to follow instructions, lack diligence, get lost in understanding the urgency of the call or be utterly ignorant of what to do. Even in such times, the ultimate failure is that of the leader, even if a weakness originated from a weak follower. The leader should lead the followers from behind to empower and encourage them to move forward.

Most ultimate failures in life start at the first step; it might be opportunities we overlook to make needed corrections; the inability to turn opportunities into strengths or to turn threats into opportunities; or the wherewithal to strengthen the weak areas using the strengths we have. In those responsibilities in which the follower appears lacking, the leader's first obligation is to empathize and lead by example, energizing the weak ones by initiating necessary actions and expecting them to follow. For the success of the team, and the leader's success, in particular, the leader must meet the ownership obligation.

Have the sense that duty must be done urgently and at any cost. Most duties of leaders are time-bound and often drive other activities in the organization. Some of the duties are critical to the organization's survival. Jim Collins in his book, *Good to Great*,[26] identified Level 5 as the highest of five levels of leadership: *Level 5 Executive-* Level leader builds enduring greatness through a paradoxical blend of personal humility, and professional will and embodies all five levels of the hierarchy. The other four levels are *Effective Leader –* characterized by a commitment to a vigorous pursuit of compelling vision; *Competent Manager*, characterized by an ability to organize people and resources toward the effective pursuit and implementation of predetermined goals and objectives; *Contributing Team Member*, characterized by an ability to personally contribute to the achievement of the group's predetermined objectives and work effectively with others in a group setting; and Highly Capable Individual, characterized by an ability to make productive contributions through talent, knowledge, skills, and good work habits.

Jesus more than exemplified the dedication to completing the work of salvation, no matter what the cost to Him. He is an immortal, omnipotent God, yet He took on the form of a mortal man and died to save and reconcile humanity to God. He did all He could possibly do, even dying on the cross.

Understand and meet the glory obligation

To understand what the glory obligation means, it is important to define what the glory of God means. The glory of God is the beauty and power that emanate from the eternal character of God in his creation, grace, providence, blessings, and redemption compared to the temporary glory of mortal man, which passes away. God created all things for His glory, including man. Man is to glorify God because man is a reflection of God; man is God's earthen vessel, which contains the glory of God. Hence, man must therefore glorify only his creator. Paul declared the same when he said, "But we have this treasure in earthen vessels, that the excellence of the power may be of God and not of us" (2 Corinthians 4:7, NKJV). Without God, man is nothing. The Bibles declares, "Everyone who is called by My name, Whom I have created for My glory; I have formed him, yes, I have made him" (Isaiah 43:7, NKJV); because the glory of man flows only from God, God has declared that He is jealous over man sharing or taking His glory elsewhere. God said, "I am the LORD, that is My name; And My glory I will not give to another, Nor My praise to carved images" (Isaiah 42:8, NKJV). The Apostle Paul also warned that man is inexcusable for exchanging the glory of the Creator (God) for the glory of the creature (man), who "Claiming to be wise, they became fools, and exchanged the glory of the immortal God for images resembling mortal" (Romans 1:22-23, ESV).

Thus, glory obligation involves understanding that glory for success belongs to God. The leader can delight and celebrate his success and those of others, but the credit or glory belongs to God. The leader can only glorify success in the Lord; that is, giving God credit for the success or seeing the success as providence from God.

To meet this obligation, we must respond in humility and seek dependence on God and His glory by following the three examples below, as well as others described in the Bible and elsewhere in this book:

1. Resist taking the glory that belongs only to God. The natural tendency for people to take glory in their accomplishments is born of human pride and the tendency to want to look better than others. A leader-servant, with his or her sense of humility, realizes that whatever he or she has accomplished is born of God's grace and wisdom. He or she resists the temptation to claim those rights, even when people assign the rights to him or her; instead, all the Glory is given to God and all praises to his or her followers.

2. Understanding the perception of God's wisdom. A leader-servant must recognize that power, and wisdom are from God. This allows the leader to remain humble in the process of meeting obligations. He or she relinquishes all rights (wisdom, values, strength) by renouncing human values; strength is gained by acknowledging his or her weakness and seeking the strength and wisdom of God because our faith is not in the wisdom of men but in the power of God (Corinthians 2:5). The things that people hold in the highest esteem are foolish in the presence of God, for "He has made foolish the wisdom of the world" (1 Corinthians 1:20, NKJV). Understanding the power of God's wisdom empowers the leader to accomplish the impossible.

3. Understanding the purpose of God's wisdom is to ensure that He gets the Glory and "that no flesh should glory in his presence" (1 Corinthians 1:29, KJV). One dangerous impact of the self-centered pursuit of glory is that it allow the devil the opportunity to use leaders to stop the movement of God. In such a case, the leader only sees his agenda and not the Gods. God called Moses "My servant" (Joshua 1:2). That same God was so angry with Moses that he did not allow him to enter the Promised Land. Why? As a leader of God's people, Moses disobeyed and disbelieved God. Instead of speaking to the rock for the immediate need of God's people (water), he struck the rock twice and cursed God's children as rebels (Numbers 20:7-11). Earlier, God told him (in Exodus 17:5) to strike the rock for water, but not in the case in Numbers 20. Moses was so blinded by his anger that he failed to see the difference that God wanted to be hallowed in the eyes of His children. Although Moses' aim was not to take or share God's glory, he failed to see the wisdom of God, and he did not reach the Promised Land.

SUMMARY 3
DEVELOPING RESPONSIBILITY-OBLIGATION

Discovering the Acts of Responsibility-Obligation

1. What is an obligation in service?
2. How can we determine the primary obligation of your calling in God's agenda? How can we meet the obligation?
3. What did the Bible teach about obligation in responsibility? (John 10:11-13; 1 Corinthians: 1:4-26; 2:1-5).

Practicing the Acts of Responsibility-Obligation

1. Responsibility-Obligation is a service or duty that a leader has committed to and to which he or she feels accountability. What are the four levels of obligation?
2. How did Apostle Paul model the the issue of obligation in responsibility the following four obligation-responsible actions:
   a. Understand and meet the purpose obligation. (1 Corinthians 1:1-5).
   b. Understand and meet your family obligations.
      (1 Corinthians 1:10-13, 1 Corinthians 12:5-6.)
   c. Understand and meet ownership obligations.
   d. Understand and meet the glory obligation (2 Corinthians 4:7)
3. With reference to responsibility leadership attribute, what take-away, meaning or lesson can you frame to improve your acts of responsibility-obligation attribute in a leadership process?
4. Write a commitment statement for plan to improve

CHAPTER 4
DEVELOPING RESPONSIBILITY-WILLINGNESS

Responsibility-willingness is the leader's willingness attitude to act responsibly. The willingness to serve is the voluntary readiness to act gladly to meet specific obligations of the positional responsibility without external pressure. Critical elements of willingness in responsibility include decisiveness, a sense of eagerness to act without pressure, enthusiasm to act with gladness, and a sense of readiness. These elements emanate from the sound value system, commitment, and motivation of the leader:

Inclination to act decisively

Indecision in a leader has serious consequences (Matthew 27: 22-31). This story of Pontius Pilate is a classic case of a leader who failed in his responsibility because he was not willing to act. Pontius Pilate, the Roman governor, was a leader who knew and understood his responsibilities, but he was not decisive. When Jesus was brought to him for judgment, he could not find anything that Jesus did wrong. However, he was still unwilling to set Him free. Here are Pilate's reasons for his indecision:

Fear of adversity and conflicts can make a leader resist taking action on an issue. Pilate had problems with his background and could not withstand adversity, which allowed conflicts to paralyze him. He knew the issues and the innocence of Jesus because he expressed no that they had handed him over because of envy. Still, he was unwilling to confront the hard issues and thus could not make a change, even though no one could explain what "evil" Jesus had done to justify His crucifixion.

Lack of self-confidence results in indecision Pilate had no confidence that any good could come from any right decision he would make. He was paralyzed by several options, and in the end, was unwilling to act. He failed in leadership because he was not willing to meet the purpose obligation.

Fear of past failures results in insecurity to act. Pilate had failed to stop the Jews rioting in the past and feared he could fail again. He allowed his past failures to define any decision as another failure because he was insecure. He had no empathy for Jesus and did not see the purpose of the good decision to set an innocent man free.

Fear of losing power and control creates a sense of unwillingness. Pilate was preoccupied with the fear of losing his control and position. This is one of the core precepts of servant leadership. Throughout human history, when a majority of people live in the sense, that they are superior to a minority group and desire to hold power; they must keep the minority group under their control. They do so by depriving them of basic rights and keeping them in bondage or feeling inferior compared to the majority. Such actions justify the majority's artificial superiority.

Lack of focus and clear perspective leaves the decision to followers. A leader must not delegate responsibility or obligation to the crowd or followers who may have a different perspective on an issue. Pilate had no focus on owner obligation. When focus and perspectives are lacking in a leader, the vision and purpose fail and thus responsibility fails. Pilate washed his hand off because he wanted to be neutral and passive over a critical issue. When a leader loses focus on where he is going, every path is an option to follow; indeed, the easiest path usually leads to failure. Thus, instead of setting Jesus free, Pilate followed the pressures of the crowd and sentenced him to death just to please the crowd. He wanted to avoid ownership of the responsibility by washing his hands of the responsibility and finally delegating the action to the crowd.

From the above examples concerning fear of adversity and conflict, we see that a lack of self-confidence, fear of past failures, fear of loss of power and control, and the lack of focus and perspective negatively impacted Pontius Pilate's willingness to take the necessary actions to meet the obligations of his responsibility to judge Jesus correctly.

Eagerness to act without external pressure

Readiness to act is the result of understanding the what, how, and when to act on an Issue. Some leaders often fail or are not eager to act because they do not understand the issue; they lack the competence or knowledge of how to act; or they simply have personal reasons for not acting. Assuming that there is a commitment to the mission and motivation for success, the following simple actions can help understand what to do and how and when to take action:

- Focus on defining the key elements of the issues: what is the purpose? What is expected? What is involved? What impact do the issues cause on the people served or the organization?
- Develop the courage to triumph over any fear that keeps you from tackling the issue.
- Ask critical questions and weigh all possible options.
- Align all the "what's" to your expected obligations and responsibilities.
- Identify your priorities and key people that can be involved in the solution; build a unified vision and consensus on the solution.
- Develop a credible plan with measurable goals, key indicators of success, and competent and trustworthy leaders to carry out the plan.

Enthusiasm to act responsibly with gladness

Understanding what is at stake and the possible action to take following the strategies above will usually increase your enthusiasm and sense of urgency on an issue within the defined scale of preference, priorities, and strategies for action. Not understanding what to do, how to do it, and when it is best to do it for the best results can be the outcome of a lack of motivation and commitment. If these are lacking and cause an unwillingness to act, then increasing commitment and motivation must be the starting point to build enthusiasm.

HOW TO INCREASE THE WILL TO ACT

To increase willfulness to act, a leader-servant that is committed and motivated to serve the people should note the following points:

1. Identify any conflicts in the issue, but see the ability to separate those conflicts from the right decision as a critical part of effective leadership.
2. Trust your judgment and have confidence in your decision based on the facts you know and on correct judgment. Understand that

just because conflicting options are difficult; this should not lead to passivity or no action on an important issue.
3. Use past experiences to build strength for the present. The fear of failure based on past failures is a recipe for failure in the present or for a legacy of failed leadership.
4. Have a sense that real power and control belong to God. People will allow the leader to focus on activities that will have a positive impact rather than focusing on activities that merely allow them to hold on to power.
5. See God as the source of strength and success and be willing to act because the fear of failure that paralyzes a leader is often caused by a sense of pride and faithlessness.
6. Emulate Jesus and the Apostle Paul, who were willing to serve by relinquishing all rights and served because of selfless love for the followers and submissive obedience to the call.
7. Do not delegate leadership responsibilities; a leader must be willing to act on an issue irrespective of the impact of the action on his position.

SUMMARY 4
DEVELOPING RESPONSIBILITY-WILLINGNESS

Discovering the Acts of Responsibility-Willingness

1. What is willingness to serve?
2. What are Critical elements of willingness in responsibility and what are the drivers of these elements?
3. Inclination to act decisively or indecision in a leader has serious consequences **as seen** ((Matthew 27: 22-31)) in the story of Pontius Pilate is a classic case of a leader who failed in his responsibility. What were Pilate's reasons for his indecision? :
4. Eagerness to act without external pressure is the result of understanding the what, how, and when to act on an Issue. What are some actions that can help you understand what to do and how and when to take action:

CHAPTER 4
DEVELOPING RESPONSIBIILITY-WILLINGNESS

Practicing the Acts of Responsibility-Willingness

1. **Responsibility-Willingness** is defined as the leader's willingness emanating from the sound value system, commitment, and motivation of the leader to act responsibly.
    a. What are your five inclinations to decisiveness to Act or ways to overcome indecision?
    b. What are your five inclinations to decisiveness to Act or ways to overcome indecision?
    c. How can leader-servant that is committed and motivated to serve the people increase willfulness to act in a purpose?
2. With reference to responsibility leadership attribute, what take-away, meaning or lesson can you frame to improve your acts of responsibility-willingness attribute in a leadership process?
3. Write a commitment statement for plan to improve .

CHAPTER 5
DEVELOPING RESPONSIBILITY-ACCOUNTABILITY

The word "accountability" is not used directly in the Bible, but one can find "give account" or "accountable" in the context of leaders being accountable for leading God's people toward God or leading them to live to please God. Accountability means being answerable to someone for the responsibility concerning an obligation. As an element of responsibility, accountability can be defined as the sense of personal ownership or liability of the obligation in leadership responsibility. We are accountable to each other, but we are ultimately accountable to God because of the sacred trust to which we must remain faithful. As in the sheep–shepherd relationship, the accountability of a leader-servant is an integral component of his responsibility to see that the flock is cared for and accounted for. Accountable leaders understand the obligations and expectations of their calling and readily accept the responsibility for any outcomes, good or bad, in meeting the obligation. Here are several Biblical examples to illustrate these points:

The follower is accountable to the leader

This means being answerable to the leader as an expression of our accountability to God by humbly submitting to the leader's authority as unto God. Paul's writing to the believers in Ephesus said, "Submit to one another out of reverence for Christ" (Ephesians 5:21). Being accountable to the leader also means the follower having confidence in them, humbly submitting to their authorities, and being answerable to what he or she is obligated. Accountability requires us to submit to God voluntarily and to one another as unto God. Submission to one another is a mutual responsibility and accountability to obedience to Christ (1 Peter 5.5). Such submission occurs from a heart willing to be humble not only to God but to each other. The ultimate result of submission is to become accountable to God. As leader-servants, a submission is an act of accountability of our obedience, respect, and honor to God rather than to each other.

The members of the flock are also stewards and they are accountable for the correct teachings they have received from the leader. Paul said a flock is to "Watch out for those who cause divisions and put obstacles in your way that are contrary to the teaching you have learned. Keep away from them (Romans 16:17, NIV), and "Remember your leaders, who spoke the word of God to you. Consider the outcome of their way of life and imitate their faith" (Hebrews 13:7, NIV).

A leader is accountable for the follower

This means being answerable to God for each member of the flock entrusted to his care. This is accomplished through teaching, support, development, and caring as a humble, selfless, obedient, and accountable leader to Christ and to others in the body of Christ. The Apostle Peter made a strong case to the elders of the church on the accountability of the shepherd over the flock. He urges them to follow Christ as their example of leadership, Servant leadership. He said, "Be shepherds of God's flock that is under your care, watching over them not because you must, but because you are willing, as God wants you to be; not pursuing dishonest gain, but eager to serve; not lording it over those entrusted to you, but being examples to the flock" (1 Peter 5:2-3, NKJV). Peter states that leaders are accountable to God for the flock under their care. They are to shepherd (guide) the sheep and watch over them because the leader is accountable to God for each member of the flock. The leaders must manage the flock entrusted to them as leader-servants by their own willingness and accountability to God to serve. Indeed, this is one of the clearest teachings on Servant leadership by any of the Apostles. God has entrusted the flock to the shepherd, and he is fully answerable to God for their physical and spiritual welfare.

A leader is accountable to God and God holds him accountable for the health of the flock. In Ezekiel 3:18, we read, "When I say to a wicked person, 'You will surely die,' and you do not warn them or speak out to dissuade them from their evil ways to save their life, that wicked person will die for their sin, and I will hold you accountable for their blood". God struck Eli dead for his failure to correct his children; indeed, Eli was accountable to God for his children's actions.

Follower-leader relational accountability

The follower and leader are accountable to each other about God. In this context, accountability means being answerable to a leader's ability to develop and nurture healthy relationships with other Christians who are pleasing to God. Such relationships also help others grow spiritually in obedience to God as a leader-servant. The followers show that they are accountable to the leader by supporting their needs and encouraging them as demonstrated by Paul, "Join me in my struggle by praying to God for me" (Romans 15:30, NIV). To those in Thessalonica Paul asked, "Now we ask you, brothers and sisters, to acknowledge those who work hard among you, who care for you in the Lord, and who admonish you. Hold them in the highest regard in love because of their work. Live in peace with each other. And we urge you, brothers and sisters, warn those who are idle and disruptive, encourage the disheartened, help the weak, be patient with everyone" (1 Thessalonians 5:12-14, NIV).

In yet another scripture, we see that the leader and the flock are all accountable to Christ. God holds the leader accountable for his responsibility for the flock, as the flock is accountable to the leader by submitting to him. They are all accountable to each other. The Bible says, "Obey those who rule over you and be submissive, for they watch out for your souls, as those who must give account (Hebrews 13:17, NKJV). The followers are to love and encourage the leaders in the accounting of them to God by submitting to their authorities. The leader must warn the weak, undisciplined, and disheartened by walking along with them, encouraging and enabling them, and above, all being patient with everyone. The leader should seek the goal of others with the ultimate goal of being accountable to Christ.

Accountability to one another is because of our relationship with God. This is what Paul addressed when he said, "So that every mouth may be silenced and the whole world held accountable to God" (Romans 3:19, NIV) and "Moreover, we have all had human fathers who disciplined us and we respected them for it. How much more should we submit to the Father of spirits and live!" (Hebrews 12:9, NIV).

SUMMARY 5
DEVELOPING RESPONSIBILITY-ACCOUNTABILITY

Discovering the Acts of Responsibility-Accountability

1. What does Accountability mean in the context of leadership? And as element of responsibility leadership?,
2. How can a follower be accountable to the Leader?
3. How can the same leader be accountable to the follower?
4. How can a Leader be accountable to God for service to the follower?

Practicing the Acts of Responsibility-Accountability

1. **Responsibility-Accountability** is defined as the sense of personal ownership or liability of the obligation in the leadership responsibility.
    a. What are some eight strategic actions a follower and the leader need to develop for a positive attitude toward accountability?
2. Accountable leaders understand the obligations and expectations of their calling and readily accept the responsibility for any outcomes, good or bad, in meeting the obligation. How do the following Biblical examples illustrate these points:
    a. The follower is accountable to the leader (Ephesians 5:21). (1 Peter 5.5; Romans 16:17; Hebrews 13:7).
    b. A leader is accountable for the follower ((1 Peter 5:2-3, Ezekiel 3:18),
    c. Follower-leader relational accountability (Romans 15:30; 1 Thessalonians 5:12-14,: Hebrews 13:17; Romans 3:19; Hebrews 12:9, NIV).
3. With reference to responsibility leadership attribute, what take-away, meaning or lesson can you frame to improve your acts of responsibility -accountability attribute in a leadership process?
4. Write a commitment statement for plan to improve.

CHAPTER 6
DEVELOPING ACCOUNTABILITY-QUALITY

Accountability quality is a measure of the culture of excellence and effectiveness in acts of accountability. Based on the scriptures above and others, followers and leaders can develop the quality of accountability by following eight strategies:

1. Cultivate a humble spirit. Humility drives submissiveness, as submissiveness is to accountability. Humans are naturally stubborn and possess a tendency to rebel against God or higher authority. As fully discussed later in Chapter 7, a humble person does not feel the need to be above or below another person and does not engage in power struggles. Hence, a humble person has no problem with submission and can, therefore, readily feel accountable to another person. As part of the quality of empathy, humility allows us to suspend or defer our judgment to submit to the will of others. Followers need to be honest and humble about their struggles in their walk with Christ and need to feel secure enough to share their vulnerabilities.

2. Cultivate a positive attitude toward accountability. Attitude is the first responsibility of a leader because it determines the attitude of success in all other aspects of leadership. All believers are accountable for their behaviors and their attitudes, reactions and actions. Leaders who desire to be great in the service of God should have someone in their lives to whom they feel accountable. This would be someone that can say, "You messed up here"—a Barnabas, who will love him enough to hold him accountable, is willing to keep him straight, and is not afraid to say, "Do not give me an excuse! You messed up." The effective mentoring of Paul by Barnabas is covered in Chapter 13 under the Encouragement Leadership Attribute.

Leadership can often be a lonely place. Even at the peak of one's leadership potential, leaders need to understand they are not infallible and have people to whom they feel accountable. Charles Swindoll was quoted in Joseph Primm's book, *Attitude in words*, as saying, "The longer I live, the more I realize the impact of attitude on life...The remarkable thing is we have a choice every day regarding the attitude we will embrace for that day. We cannot change our past... we cannot change the fact that people will act in a certain way. And so it is with you... we are in charge of our Attitudes." [27] Ultimately, we are accountable for any outcome of the choices we make and our responses toward life issues, no matter the challenges we face. Our accountabilities must therefore involve developing positive attitudes toward others.

3. Do all things to the Glory of God! When our attitude is to live a life pleasing, and have an attitude of accountability to God, we will invariably show accountability to a leader who also is answerable to God. A leader can provide needed discipleship through Bible study to share what the word means and how to apply it; prayers said together in good and bad times; sharing testimonies; and knowing how each member is dealing with their challenges. These are essential activities in this model. Be patient and understanding with everyone and correct each other in love.

4. Develop measurable goals and objectives to guide your life and service. This strategy involves establishing and communicating expectations for accountability. You are only answerable to what you know; leaders and followers cannot be held accountable for what they do not know. Developing measurable goals and objectives begins by defining each person's expectations and responsibilities clearly. Effectiveness in accomplishing a set of goals often depends on the buy-in of all involved. Hence, it is important to involve all stakeholders, especially when there is a need to raise standards of expectations. Leaders and followers must avoid the temptation to assume that people know what to do. Once the goals are defined, and the expectations are communicated clearly, efforts should be made to provide training for people who do not know how to do their assigned tasks. Organizations increase performance in what they measure, and such measurement records the accountability of what was expected. It is important to identify things such as the quality of Bible study, growth in spiritual involvement, increase and retention of membership, and commitment to increased responsibilities. Leaders' responsibilities are meant not only to influence a desired change by communicating to followers what to do and ensuring instructions were followed, but also to make intentional efforts to oversee the followers' performance, completion, and personal growth in the project.

5. Develop trust in each other. Developing trust means building unity of purpose. It means trusting that our accountability is ultimate to God. Admittedly, there is an element of confidentiality in accountability because of our human frailties. A brother who is struggling with an aspect of his walk with the Lord and who has a sense of accountability to another brother or the leader can see any sharing is a sacred trust. This means the individuals equally submit to each other as they do unto the Lord by effectively holding themselves accountable for the same values, beliefs, truths, expectations, and mutual interest in being accountable to God. As Paul said to the Corinthian leaders; asking them to forsake the division among them; "Be perfectly joined together in the same mind and the same judgment" (1 Corinthians 1:10, KJV).

6. Be faithful in entrusted things. The flock of God is entrusted to a leader-servant who is expected to remain faithful in accounting for the well-being of the flock. Paul described the nature of accountability of apostleship when he said, "This, then, is how you ought to regard us: as servants of Christ and as those entrusted with the mysteries God has revealed. Now it is required that those who have been given a trust must prove faithful" (1 Corinthians 4:1-2, NIV). We exhibit accountability to the teachings entrusted to us by answering to the correct use of such teachings or by adhering to the truth of the teachings. It is part of accountability for faithful leader-servants to entrust sacred things, caring for the flock, the teachings, the values, and the revelations to the service of God. In instructing Timothy regarding what he has learned of accountability, Paul said, "And the things that you have heard from me among many witnesses, commit these to faithful men who will be able to teach others also" (2 Timothy 2:2, NKJV).

7. Serve as a living sacrifice. Paul taught that we are accountable to God for the way we live our lives. Each person must give an account of his life as a living sacrifice to God. Paul said, "Therefore, I urge you, brothers and sisters, in view of God's mercy, to offer your bodies as a living sacrifice, holy and pleasing to God—this is your true and proper worship" (Romans 12:1, NIV). Offering our "bodies as a living sacrifice" means to present our entire bodies willingly (all parts of our whole selves)—without the assumptions of any right—as one living sacrifice to God. In other words, we engage in active devotion to honor God completely as if we have no other rights. A sacrifice has no rights, so we are to present our whole self as an active sacrifice that is holy and acceptable to God. A sacrifice is totally accountable, pure, and holy (acceptable) to God. This is the minimum reasonable service we can do and all to the glory of God.

8. Develop a sense of public accountability. Leaders are often the reflections through which the public sees an organization; indeed, leaders' moral failures can negatively impact their followers and the organization. Despite David's moral failure, he valued public accountability and charged all leaders under him to follow the ways of God. He said, "So now I charge you in the sight of all Israel and of the assembly of the LORD, and in the hearing of our God: Be careful to follow all the commands of the LORD your God" (1 Chronicles 28:8, NIV). Through a sense of public accountability, leaders intentionally subject themselves to public scrutiny as a measure of their actions. It serves as a humble way to solicit the opinion of the flock or allow others to share in decision-making. A sense of public accountability is a call to the public or the flock. In the cases of David and Nehemiah, for example, both sought to project God's presence in everything. Public accountability is a leader's way to involve others to see his or her transparency and accountability. Paul made this point to the Corinthian church: that they must hold each other accountable for how they conduct their lives.

REASONS FOR ESTABLISHING ACCOUNTABILITY

Based on the Work of Bill Hull in *The Disciple Making Pastor*, [28] J. Hampton Keathley, III made several key points on leadership accountability in a series of articles titled "Marks of Maturity: Biblical Characteristics of a Christian Leader." [29] Included were the following five reasons for establishing accountability:

1. Accountability is an essential part of a functional society. The prototype for accountability is the triune Godhead itself. The Spirit accepts His role as the enabler or comforter to come and dwell in believers. The Son accepts His role as the suffering Savior of the world, first by becoming true humanity that He might die for our sins,

CHAPTER 6
DEVELOPING ACCOUNTABILITY-QUALITY

and then, as our advocate, by sitting at God's right hand. Accountability helps promote Biblical checks and balances. It provides the necessary discipline and support to see people reach Godly goals. God has given the Word and the Holy Spirit as His agents to help provide direction and control of our lives. Accountability to other believers becomes another key instrument to aid self-discipline and inner control.

2. Accountability promotes servant-like leadership in keeping with the pastoral mandate to watch over the flock. One of the key requirements of a leader-servant is faithfulness to the things entrusted to him (1 Corinthians 4:1-2) and to entrust what he has learned to faithful men (2 Timothy 2:2). Accountability is necessary because, like sheep, we tend to go our own way. Making disciples means teaching others to obey the Lord; this is very difficult without some measure of accountability.

3. Accountability protects both leaders and the flock. The Biblical model for church leadership is the leadership of elders who provide a structure for accountability. In this structure, the flock submits to its leaders, because the leaders keep watch over the souls of God's people. The goal of accountability is to help people grow in Christ and learn to find Him as the source, force, and course of life.

SUMMARY 6
DEVELOPING ACCOUNTABILITY-QUALITY

Discovering the Acts of Accountability-Quality

1. What is Accountability quality?
2. How did the Bible support the follow strategies followers and leaders can adopt to develop the quality of accountability
    a. Cultivate a positive attitude toward accountability.
    b. Do all things to the Glory of God!
    c. Develop trust in each other. (1 Corinthians 1:10, KJV).
    d. Be faithful in entrusted things. (1 Corinthians 4:1-2, NIV). (2 Timothy 2:2, NKJV).
    e. Serve as a living sacrifice. (Romans 12:1, NIV).
    f. Develop a sense of public accountability. the commands of the LORD your God" (1 Chronicles 28:8, NIV).

Practicing the Acts of Accountability-Quality

1. **Accountability-quality** is a measure of the culture of excellence and effectiveness or competence in acts of accountability.
    a. Based on the works of other leaders, Biblical Characteristics of a Christian Leader." what are the reasons for establishing accountability in leadership?
2. What did Apostle teach about how being accountable promotes servant-like leadership in keeping with the pastoral mandate (1 Corinthians 4:1-2; (2 Timothy 2:2).
3. Why is Accountability necessary in effective discipleship?
4. With reference to responsibility leadership attribute, what take-away, meaning or lesson can you frame to improve your acts of responsibility-quality attribute in a leadership process?
5. Write a commitment statement for plan to improve

TOPIC INDEX

About This Book, 22
accountability, 77, 79, 83, 84, 86
   confidentiality, 83
   developing, 60, 80, 81, 85
Accountability, 85, 86
   definition, 77, 80
   public, 84, 85
   reasons for, 84
   to another, 79
accountability to God, 82
Accountable
   to God, 78, 80
Affective Compassion, 77
authentic, 24, 26
authentic leadership, 37
Authentic Leadership, 45
Authenticity, 43
characteristics of responsibility attribute, 58
Comfort, 41
commitment, 19, 25, 59, 71, 75, 82
communication
   types of, 30
Communication, 30
Comparisons
   with other works, 40
Compassion, 28
credibility, 48
David, 84
dependence on God, 68
develop responsibility attributes, 61, 69
Developing responsibility attribute
   Meet the Glory-Obligation, 67
   meet the Ownership-Obligations, 65, 69
   Meet the Purpose-Obligation, 62, 69
   Meet your Family-Obligation, 64, 69
Developing Willingness to Act, 71, 74
Empathy-attribute, 28
Emulate, 74
expectations, 77, 80, 83
focus
   lack of, 72
Functional Definitions, 35
giving, 67
How to Increase the Will to Act, 73
humility, 68, 81
Inclination to Decisiveness to Act, 60, 71, 74, 75

Initiative
   definition of, 29
inside-out, 46
John C. Maxwell, 55
Joshua, 19, 62
law of, 42
LEADER, 28
Leader as Servant Leadership, 42
   definition, 25
Leader First., 23
Leader-as-Servant Leadership, 23
leader-servant's affection-attribute
   definition, 48
leadership, 25
Leadership Attributes, 43
Leadership Inner Value system, 25
Leadership responsibility attribute
   definition of, 58, 60
Model, 23
moral capital, 56
Moses, 19, 68
Navigation-attribute, 48
Obligation-Responsibility, 69
Personal Outward Authenticity, 47
Practicing Servant Leadership
   Responsibility, 60
process, 25
reasons for establishing accountability, 84
relationships, 79
Responsibility- Willingness-, 74, 75
sacrifice,, 83
selfless, 74
sense of purpose, 64
Servant, 23, 24
Servant leadership responsibility principle, 58
Strategies for Developing Accountability, 85
submission, 79
suffering, 84
Teachable Moments to Grow, 80
test
   for leader-servant authenticity, 46
   of essential elements of personal authenticity, 46, 47
The Leadership Influence-attribute, 41
The Principle of Leadership Responsibility-attribute, 52, 60

ALS RESPONSIBILITY LEADERSHIP ATTRIBUTES, PRINCIPLES, & PRACTICES

The Principle of Leadership Empathy-Attribute, 28
The Principle of Leadership Adaptability Attribute, 27
The Principle of Leadership listening-attribute, 30

Timothy, 83, 85, 86
Trust, 83, 85
will of God, 62
willingness, 56, 59, 71, 74, 78

REFERENCES

[1] Greenleaf, R. (1970). *The Servant as Leader,* Indianapolis: The Robert K. Greenleaf Center

[2] Spears, L. (1996*).* "*Reflections on Robert K. Greenleaf and servant-leadership.*" Leadership & Organization Development Journal, 17(7), 33-35

[3] Russell, R.F. (2001). "The role of values in servant leadership." *Leadership & Organization Development Journal,* 22(2), 76-83

[4] Russell, R.F., and Stone, A.G. (2002). "A review of servant leadership attributes: developing a practical model." *Leadership & Organization Development Journal,* 23(3), 145-15

[5] Terry. R. W (1993*). Authentic Leadership: Courage In Action,* San Francisco, CA, Jossey-Bass

[6] George, B (2003). *Authentic Leadership: Rediscovering the Secrets to Creating Lasting Value.* San Francisco, CA, Jossey-Bass

[7] Shamir, B. & Eilam, G. (2005). "What's your story? Toward a life-story approach to authentic leadership." Leadership Quarterly, 16, 395–418.

[8] Anderson, GL (2009). *Advocacy Leadership: Toward a Post-Reform Agenda in Education*, Routledge, New York, 41

[9] Yacobi, B.G. *"Elements of Human Authenticity."* http://www.philosophytogo.org/wordpress/?p=1945, Retrieved, July 15, 2012

[10] George, B (2003). *Authentic Leadership: Rediscovering the Secrets to Creating Lasting Value*, San Francisco, CA, Jossey-Bass

[11] Wosu, SN (2014), *Leader as Servant Leadership Model,* Xulon Press

[12] Slater, R (2002), *29 Leadership Secrets From Jack Welch*, McGraw Hill Professional Publisher

[13] Cameron, K.S., & Caza, A. (2005). "Developing strategies for responsible leadership." In J. Doh & S. Stumph (Eds.), *Handbook on responsible leadership and governance in global business* (pp. 87-111). New York: Oxford University Press

[14] Denison, D. R. (1996), "What is the difference between organizational culture and organizational climate? A native's point of view on a decade of paradigm wars", Academy of Management Review, 21(3), 619-654

[15] Smidts, A., A. T. H. Pruyin & C. B. M. Van Riel (2001),"The impact of employee communication and perceived external prestige on organizational identification", Academy of Management Journal, 44(5), 1051-1062.

[16] Fredrickson, B. L. (2002), "Positive emotions", in C. R. Snyder, & S. J. Lopez (eds), Handbook of Positive Psychology, New York, NY: Oxford University Press, pp. 120-134.

[17] Fredrickson, B. L. (2003), "Positive emotions and upward spirals in organizations", in K. S. Cameron, J. E. Dutton & R. E. Quinn (eds), Positive Organizational Scholarship, San Francisco, CA: Berrett-Koehler Publishers Inc., pp. 163-175. 16

[18] Staw, B. M. & S. G. Barsade (1993), "Affect and managerial performance: A test of the sadder-but-wiser versus happier-and-smarter hypotheses", Administrative Science Quarterly, 38, 304-331. 18

[19] Isen, A. M. (1987), "Positive affect, cognitive processes, and social behavior", Advances in Experimental Social Psychology, 20, 203-253

[20] Kanov, J.M., S. Maitlis, M.C. Worline, J.E., Dutton, P.J. Frost, & J.M. Lilius (2004) "Compassion in organizational life." American Behavioral Scientist, 47, 808-827.

[21] Wrzesniewski, A. (2003), "Finding positive meaning in work", in K. S. Cameron, J. E. Dutton & R. E. Quinn (eds), Positive Organizational Scholarship, San Francisco, CA: Berrett-Koehler Publishers Inc., pp. 296-308.

[22] Maxwell, JC (2007). *Talent is Never Enough, Thomas Nelson*

[23] On Point Consulting (2008). "Build a Culture of Accountability: Five Ways to Enhance the Level of Accountability", NY, Aug. 18, PR Newswire, New York. http://www.reuters.com/article/2008/08/18/idUS75054+18-Aug-2008+PRN20080818

[24] Pratt, M. G. & B. E. Ashforth (2003), 'Fostering meaningfulness in working at work', in K. S. Cameron, J. E. Dutton & R. E. Quinn (eds.), Positive Organizational Scholarship, San Francisco, CA: Berrett-Koehler Publishers Inc., pp. 309-327.

[25] Hackman, J. R. & G. R. Oldham (1980), Work design, Reading, MA: Addison-Wesley.

[26] Collins, Jim (2001) *Good to Great: Why Some Companies Make the Leap… and Others Don't*, HarperBusiness

[27] Primm, J (2008). *Attitude in Words*, Publisher Lulu, P. 136
[28] Bill Hull, *The Disciple Making Pastor*, Fleming H. Revell, Old Tappan, New Jersey, 1988, p. 159.
[29] Keathley, J. H, III, Marks of Maturity: Biblical Characteristics of a Christian Leader , Mark #16: Accountability, https://bible.org/seriespage/mark-16-accountability. Retrieved, July 2012

www.ingramcontent.com/pod-product-compliance
Lightning Source LLC
LaVergne TN
LVHW050025080526
838202LV00069B/6914